Greenacre Writers Anthology

Greenacre Writers Short Story Competition 2013

Editors
Lindsay Bamfield
Rosie Canning

Judge
Alex Wheatle

Greenacre Project

First published 2014 by
The Greenacre Project
25 Chislehurst Avenue
London N12 0HU
website: www.greenacreproject.blogspot.co.uk

ISBN 978-0-9569914-2-3

A catalogue record for this book is available
from the British Library

Printed in Great Britain by CPI London, London

Editors' Introduction

"Short stories are tiny windows into other worlds and other minds and other dreams. They are journeys you can make to the far side of the universe and still be back in time for dinner." Neil Gaiman.

Our third anthology comprises the winning stories from our third Short Story competition and work from members of The Greenacre Writers. We were very honoured to have Alex Wheatle as our competition judge.

> 'I thoroughly enjoyed poring over the short-list for the Greenacre Writers prize and found the standard of storytelling very high. I hope that every writer who is included in this anthology will gain confidence and a great boost to fuel their writing career. I'd like to take this opportunity to wish every author the best for the future and to thank Ms Rosie Canning and Ms Lindsay Bamfield for trusting me and letting me loose on the shortlist.'
>
> Alex Wheatle, MBE

When he selected the winners Alex said: 'I had to read the short list three times because it's so difficult picking a winner! I chose 'Flapjack' as the winner. It was an original piece of writing and I loved the author's brave approach to a very difficult subject matter. 'Colours Fade to Black and White' came in second place. I loved the young narrator's voice and the author created some wonderful characters in this short piece. In third place was 'Tingalay-o' - the prose in this short story's opening is stunning and throughout the piece. I loved the style of writing and was moved by the end.'

Greenacre Writers, based in Finchley, North London, comprises novelists, autobiographers, short story writers and poets, and we offer a selection of our work, chosen by the individual authors. As with our competition winners, we encompass a variety of genres and styles in our stories from fantasy to contemporary, from poetic to gritty. Greenacre Writers encourages new talent and we are delighted that this anthology and the two previous editions have enabled the first publication for some writers.

Lindsay Bamfield and Rosie Canning, March 2014

Flapjack

17ᵗʰ July

7.46pm - 3 eggs.

I'm waiting. They usually come in sixes. Or twelves. Jade's upstairs. Hopefully got her earphones in. So hot. I hate summer. The kids stay out longer, which means we're both stuck in here. I hate having to keep windows shut, draw curtains and sit in with the television on. I've turned the volume right up, a sitcom with canned laughter.

8.02pm - 3 more eggs.

I heard them splat against the window. The yolks and whites will be running down the glass. Not a very interesting book I'm writing. Eggs, eggs, flour, tinned tomatoes and spaghetti. Eggs, beans, eggs and more eggs. Just write down what they say and do. Keep a record of dates and times. That's what I was told. I'm glad these notebooks were 'buy one get one free' so I can write more in this second one.

Jade was going through the bathroom cabinet before. I asked her what she was looking for. She said 'nothing' and started tidying it away. She said she was sorting the cupboard out. Very suspicious. She doesn't even tidy her own room without prompting. I'll make her favourite omelette tonight. Cheese and mushroom.

8.56pm - 'We're gonna get you, ya fucking fat bitches.' More eggs and something heavy hit the window. Don't know what it is.

That was loud. Don't think the window broke this time. At least the car they set fire to has gone this week.

I asked Jade did she want something putting on the shopping list but she just shrugged. I heard the pring of her phone. I'm glad she's in touch with her mates in the holidays though she doesn't go out much. I asked if she was going to look at her message. She just said 'later' and went back upstairs. She spends a lot more time in her room here but she'll be fourteen next year. Won't want to hang out with me at all soon.

9.02pm - Tinned spaghetti thrown at the front door and living room window. I looked out, tried to not let them see me. They shouted 'Fat Cow' when they saw me at the window. Then 'Fucking Fat Bitches,' over and over.

Nothing's been the same since we had to move. This wouldn't have happened in Greenacres. There were more places for kids to go round there. That bastard, Dave. I can understand him leaving me but what about her? She's his daughter and he can't even phone or send something for her birthday.

9.20pm - They're in the garden of the empty house. Four of them, two Hegleys, two others. The one with the red jacket.

9.32pm - More pasta and eggs, thrown at the kitchen window. I shut the blind. Shouting but I couldn't hear what. Loud music on TV.

I'm sure they make the adverts louder. I didn't want to hear what they were shouting but I'm supposed to write it down.

10.22pm - Tomatoes and cakes. Two of them came through the gate and squashed cakes into the letterbox. 'Fucking fat bitches' a few times through the letterbox.

They could see me standing in the hall. Cake is a new one. I watched it land on the mat. I wanted to do something but didn't know what. I've been told not to speak to them again. Just supposed to stay indoors and write it down.
   It's three weeks since I went out and told them to leave us alone. They just laughed. I wish I hadn't said anything. Got worse since. They started throwing the tins. That's when I called the police. Two days peace we had till they came back.
   I'm sure Dave's mum knows his new number. She doesn't care about her grand-daughter. Makes me think of me and Gran and all the times I stayed with her. I wish Jade could've had that. It's been horrible for her recently, starting senior

school and having to move to a new one after one term.

I'm in bed now. Jade was still on her laptop when I looked in. I told her to switch off and get some sleep.

18th July

8.14pm - They're out there again, arrived later tonight. Messing about in next door's garden, pretending to fight with the planks from the fence. Three Hegleys this time, the older brother too. And the one with the red jacket and the little blond one. They were shouting and laughing but I don't think it was directed at us.

Jade went out early. She was gone all morning. When she came back she said she'd been shopping. I could see from the bags she'd been to Superdrug and Wilkies. I told her I could've got whatever she needed from Asda. 'Your shampoo was on offer,' she said. I asked if she wanted the money. She just shrugged and went upstairs.

She only came down when I called her for tea. Spaghetti Bolognese. I make it from scratch with carrots and mushrooms, a glug of red wine and lots of garlic. Most people these days buy a jar and just add to the meat but that's not the same. Jade likes it with lots of cheese melted on top. It seemed to cheer her up. Me too. Even scooping spaghetti and tomatoes up from the doorstep and scraping it off the windows doesn't put me off.

8.36pm - Eggs - 6 all at once.

I notice they've left the box in our hedge.

We stay in more now. When going out involves getting past at least three boys calling names after you down the street and everyone staring, you tend to do that. Did the supermarket shop at one in the morning last week. I waited till they left, then went out and got a taxi. Bought anything that was on offer and lots of basics and tinned stuff. Not much left of this month's money but we're well stocked up.

8.55pm - 9.04pm - Flour, more eggs and beans.

Got to draw the curtains now. I have to crawl on the floor, slowly reach up and hope they don't notice. Just went and made coffee. Jade's taken the Jaffa Cakes upstairs again. She was rooting through the junk drawer in the kitchen after tea. What's she looking for? She received a lot of texts tonight. She never looks happy to get them though. Don't think she even bothers replying.

She was on her laptop most of the evening. I wish she'd stay down here with me. She used to sit downstairs more at the old place. Showed me all the stuff she looked up online for that North Pole project she did before Christmas. She showed me the forum where she was talking about *Hollyoaks* with someone in Dundee and the photo she put on Facebook. It's the one Dave took of her in the New Forest last summer. A boiling hot, two-ice-cream day. Her face is all red from sunburn but she looks really happy. She's wearing that orange tie-dye top. She's outgrown that now.

Jade thinks it's her they're shouting at. I keep telling her it's me but we know it's both of us. I once asked if anyone ever said anything at school and she said no straight away. Maybe it's different these days. Well, bullying's talked about more now. That's the impression I get from television.

I went into Jade's room just now. She slammed the laptop shut. I asked if she was all right. She said 'fine' and hugged me goodnight. I thought she'd stopped doing that. I suggested we go out tomorrow. Get the train into town. Go shopping. Put it on the credit card. Treat ourselves for the holidays. Go to the Italian for pizza and a sundae. Even though it isn't Sunday I said, like we always say. She just shrugged and gave a little half-smile. I said, 'we'll see in the morning'.

10.03pm - 12 Eggs. Laughing. Usual names - Fat bitches, fat cow, fat pigs, sometimes with 'fucking' in front, sometimes without. Went on until …

10.12pm - The older brother turned up in a car, they all piled in and left.

You'd think they could find something better to do. And why is it always animals? Is it such an insult? I like animals. People say 'chicken', 'what a bunch of sheep' and 'rat' as well.

They've probably gone up to Asda to nick some more

supplies. Mr Mistry told me he won't let them in his shop anymore. I hate having to go out early to clean up. I scoop the food up with the dustpan. The smell of raw eggs and spaghetti mixed together makes me feel sick. I knock it into doubled-up carrier bags and tie them tightly. Bits of shell get stuck in the bristles and I have to wash the brush and pan. Then I fill a bucket with hot water, mop the step, wipe the windows down and polish them. That's my morning routine these days. Before Jade gets up and before the people next door on the other side see.

I've had this idea. Give them a taste of their own medicine. I would get a load of syrup and warm it gently. Not so hot it'll burn, just enough to make it runny. There'd be buckets of it on the windowsill in my bedroom. I'd take one bucket of the syrup outside earlier, pour a layer on the path and flowerbed. I'd get boxes and boxes of porridge oats and cheap rice krispies and a few pots of those horrible sticky clown's-nose cherries. Jade loves those. I'd have them ready on the bed behind me. Then I'd wait till they arrive. I'd have to get them to come near the house. I'd pull back the curtains and put the light on. That would make them come over.

I'd be ready, waiting for the right moment before opening the window. Their laughter, swearing and jeering stirring up my stomach, spurring me on. As fast as I could, I'd pour the syrup over them. They'd probably start to run away, feet getting stuck on the path. Then I'd get the catapult I'd constructed earlier. I'm not sure how I'd do that. Perhaps I borrowed Jade's laptop and googled catapults. I'd fill the big plastic bowl with the oats and krispies and fire them out of the window to land on their heads. They'd stick to the syrup in their hair. Then, I'm sure they'd be out of the gate by now, hopefully there'd be enough time to send the clown's noses after the rest.

Then it would be *me* laughing at *them*. At the window, just laughing at them with helmets of that sticky, oaty, crispy mess setting on their heads. I'd still be laughing later, thinking of all the other kids laughing and then their families laughing when they get home. Imagine having to wash that out! They'd be picking off cherries and pulling clumps of hair-flapjack off their heads. They'd be trying to shower it off with the hot water melting the syrup and soggy cherry porridge collecting in the plughole. They'd have to scoop it out or it would clog up the drains. Hope their dads give them a slap instead of giving *me* dirty looks whenever I try to suggest they speak to their sons about how rude they are to my daughter.

Of course I wouldn't do this. The police community support officer would have something to say. Just keep a record, she says. Dates and times. Yes, it'd be me in trouble and I'm sure no one would even notice me saying 'They started it.' A childish thing to say, I know. But they did.

They've not been back yet. It's gone eleven now. I've just called Jade to see if she wants a drink. No answer.

She's probably listening to her music. I'll read her my flapjack idea tomorrow.

I'm quite proud.

Colours Fade to Black and White

My life seems to be made up of spinning yo-yos. There they go in a kaleidoscope of colours like the stained glass in next door's window. Pinks, purples, yellows, reds and greens. This is my world.

We have steamed vegetables for tea. They arrived earlier today in a bio-degradable easily-to-fold-down box. All organic, of course and so fresh they hardly take any cooking. Mum doesn't buy supermarket vegetables. She says it's like eating plastic and goodness only knows how long they've been in transit.

We don't eat meat in this house. As far as Mum is concerned, I've never eaten meat, but I couldn't resist trying a bacon roll at Casey's house once and another time a tuna mayo sandwich. It was what everyone else was having and I didn't want to make a fuss or to be different from the others.

As I sit eating my corn-on-the-cob, melted butter dripping down my chin, I think about Delith Jones. She hadn't long joined our school before she was abducted. I liked her dark curly hair and goofy teeth. She was kind to me.

Now I can't step outside the front door without Mum or Dad asking where I'm going and who with. They have a five step policy in place; things I have to do if I'm suspicious of anyone. The one I won't be able to do is to kick him in the wotsits. I mean, he'd just grab my leg, wouldn't he and then he'd see my knickers and he'd have won.

They still haven't found Delith, nor her body. At school we imagine what could have become of her. Anita says she thinks she's been strangled and dumped in the river. Casey says she's still alive and being kept in a locked-up shed at the bottom of someone's garden, and Paul Mallander says she's been battered to death with a brick.

I think a man and a lady who can't have babies and IVF hasn't worked for them have taken her to be their special little girl. Delith's probably wearing Mini Boden clothes and attending tap and ballet lessons in Primrose Hill like my cousin. A better life than this boring old town.

Mum says never to talk to strangers, but if I listened to

her, then I'd never have made friends with Mr Timms at Number 53, nor his Polish lodgers who have very red faces and deep voices.

I'm sitting on the front garden wall waiting for Dad to come home and I'm playing with next door's tabby cat. Shilough, he's called. He spends more time at our house than next door. Mum says it's because they're rubbish pet owners and leave him locked outside most of the day. I pick long stalks of grass and flick them around to tease him. He seems to like that and plays for ages. When Mum's not looking I pour some full fat organic milk into an old bowl and give it to Shilough. She's told me hundreds of times not to encourage him, but he's so sweet, I can't resist and I'm sure next door don't feed him properly. Not Mr Timms at Number 53. The other side. The Whites.

Mr White is always in the corner shop buying firelighters. I had to ask Mum what they were. She said they were white blocks you put on an open fire to keep it from going out. I like the black box they come in. It has pretty orange flames on it. Mr White has whitish-grey hair and bright twinkly blue eyes. He never says hello and he shuffles. I've never seen him wearing shoes, only slippers; tartan ones with cream edging.

Mum says the Whites have a hoarding problem. I'm not really sure what that is, but their windows are dirty and they always have the curtains closed so you can't see inside. Mum says all sorts could be going on in there and no one would ever know.

For a moment I wonder whether Delith Jones is in there.

Mum says the Whites' property would be worth a fortune, if they did it up. They have a four-bedroom Victorian house like ours on the outskirts of town with all its original features. She says if it was renovated like ours, then it would be worth at least £600,000. I can't imagine that much money. Lots of weekly shops, and super deluxe veg boxes from Wild and Free Organics, anyway.

'Don't go wandering off!' Mum shouts from the front door. 'Bath time in ten minutes!'

That means at least twenty. She'll either be texting Auntie Carole or having a sneaky glass of wine before Dad gets home. Or both.

Shilough lies down so that I can tickle his belly. I do it with a stalk of grass, because my hands go all blotchy and red if I touch his fur. I get that from Dad. It's why we can't have a cat of our own, he says.

I hear the Whites' front door slam and look up.

Mrs White levers herself down the front steps. Mum says she's a martyr to her arthritis. She has a brown and red checked shopping bag over her arm. She never speaks and always looks at the floor. Her hair is dyed a weird orangey colour, as if she's left the dye on too long or something. She ignores Shilough, and he doesn't seem bothered.

When she turns the corner, I dare myself to run to their front door and lift the letterbox. It's something I've been trying to do for ages. I just want to peer into their hallway to see the newspapers and old milk cartons; to see if what Mum says is true. It's so dark in there, though, I can't see a thing. I fiddle around in my pocket till I find what I need.

My heart is thrumming like the old traction engines Dad took me to see at the steam fair last week. I look left and right, then just as I'm lifting the letterbox, I see a shadow pass by the window and I shiver. Someone is watching me. My mouth goes dry and it tastes like I've been munching on metal. For a moment I'm frozen; as if my feet are cemented into the floor. I feel as if I'm going to wet myself, then I hear Shilough's miaow, which makes everything seem normal and safe. I turn from the door and run back to our garden. I should go inside now, but I want to see what happens.

Dad will be home from work any minute now. I start looking for his bike. He always cycles to work. The only time we use the car is for holidays and weekend trips to visit family. Anita's mum calls us 'eco-warriors' whatever they are. Dad says we're Green.

It's then I hear a tap-tapping on the window. I turn around expecting to see Mum calling me in. Tap tap-tap. I can't see Mum's face at the window. Then I look next door.

The Whites' curtain is twitching and I see a fist at the window. Tap tap-tap.

I stay on our side of the path and walk a little closer to the window. I can see a smudgy shape through the thin curtain. It's probably creepy Mr White. I remember Mum and Dad's five step policy regarding strangers. The first step is to run into our house as fast I can, if I'm near home, that is.

My legs won't move.

The fist isn't big enough for Mr White's. It's a child's fist knocking the window, I'm sure.

'Molly! Inside now!' Mum shouts.

I should do as I'm told, but I need to know if it really is Delith Jones knocking at the window. Perhaps the Whites have half-buried her beneath piles of old newspapers and plastic milk cartons?

I creep closer; as close as I dare. I can see an orangey glow through the curtains, then smoke. Someone is coughing; choking even.

Mr White and his firelighters. A box every day. Why does he need so many? What if he's bought them to help set his house on fire and burn the evidence?

I hear a bicycle bell behind me and Dad's waving and grinning like a loony. Suddenly everything seems less scary.

'What are you doing spying on the Whites, Molly, love?'

I put my fingers to my lips and call him over. I can smell the smoke now and the orange glow is brighter. I feel excited and wonder whether I'll see that kaleidoscope of colours I see when Dad has a bonfire in the back garden. I'm just about to ask him, but he's busy talking into his Iphone.

I never did get to have a bath that night. Mum said it was far too late by the time the fire brigade had gone.

Delith's parents bought me a big cuddly cat and a box of chocolates. I can't understand why, because I didn't do anything.

Mr and Mrs White don't live next door anymore.

Mum says they're in custody, whatever that means. Perhaps they live in a world that's yellow and thick.

The RSPCA man was nice, but he said I couldn't keep Shilough. Maybe Dad told him about my rash.

I accidentally told Casey's mum and dad about the matches when they were feeding me more bacon sandwiches one Saturday morning. I only fed two through the letter box so that I could see inside a bit better.

They promised not to tell.

There isn't a kaleidoscope of colours next door now. The door is charred black against the white walls and now the Whites have gone, so have my spinning yo-yos and my world is a dull shade of grey.

Tingalay-o

Silvery grey drizzle fell into the murky November dawn. The heavy, slow-moving cloud cover was unwilling to relinquish its obscurity to a new day. Light hoarfrost had settled quietly in the night but now the slight rise in temperature and the wet air was beginning to obliterate the beauty of the glittering chill. Wraithlike trees were returning to their dank wintry sleepiness as they dripped dark bitter tears on to the brittle floor beneath. The fairy dell setting was washed away to reveal pedestrian wet grass compacted with the past season's discarded pine needles.

Apart from the systematic drip from the forestry and the occasional hiss of tyres on the wet road from sporadic early morning traffic, the air was still silent. The over-wintering birds had decided it was not yet time to kick start the small plantation into life and the small nocturnal mammals had shuffled off into safer depths well before the first signs of morning. The girl stood motionless behind the concealing trunk of a tall pine. She had positioned herself as far into the wood as she could whilst still keeping the timber toilet block on the edge of the car park in her line of sight. For a seventeen year old who had just given birth it had been a long vigil but she could not leave yet.

She was grateful that the night had been dry when she arrived, already in labour. The trek across three fields had been arduous. She still felt dangerously too close to home but it was the best her weary body could manage and she had to return before she was missed. She had gleaned her knowledge of the birth process from the internet, even watching a video on YouTube, and had planned her confinement with impressive precision. In theory she knew how to cut the cord and deal with the afterbirth. She was not after all a high flying scholar for nothing. When she considered the unthinkable alternative, she had, despite her terror, convinced herself she could manage the ordeal. She had even decided that death would be preferable to exposure and so to die in the course of delivering would be merciful.

However, as the girl soon discovered, technology for all its extensive and encyclopaedic expertise was not so great at depicting pain, nor was childbirth however excruciating and unattended a predictable gateway to oblivion. For hours she alternated from tossing on a groundsheet to stumbling round the protective circle of trees, clinging to the coarse bark until her fingers bled, screaming away her lonely anguish to the night sky. As the temperature fell and the first frost formed she was warmed by the sweat of her physical exertions and in her agony she begged aloud for help. So well had she chosen her location that the only response to her painful cries was from an owl who howled away unseen, in disturbed unison.

When she felt the urge to push and the effort relieve her tearing torture she calmed and braced herself, knowing that she was approaching the dramatic finale. She felt for the head as it crowned and gently eased the daughter she would never know into the world. She rested, warming the yelling baby momentarily with her own body's heat before wrapping her securely in layers of warm blankets. The child soon settled against her breasts and slept as the very young and innocent manage to do so easily. She wiped the child's tawny skin and wrinkled old lady's face and gazed upon the exquisite beauty only a new mother sees.

In her post-natal exhaustion the girl was reluctant to move but with her primordial hormones raging, her maternal instinct was to protect the new life she had produced. She padded her sore and bleeding body and pulled on her warm coat cocooning the infant inside to radiate extra warmth. She felt consoled by the closeness and her tired mind stored away the brief precious connection. As she walked out of the trees towards the toilet block she rocked the oblivious bundle in her arms singing softly as her mother had once sung to her; 'Tingalay-o, come me little donkey, come.'

She went through the entrance to the female toilets where she placed the child gently in the sink and settled her tenderly. She placed an envelope behind the cold tap.

Now she was watching and waiting. If someone didn't come soon she would not be able to resist the urge to go back and check on the baby. If that happened she was not convinced she would have the strength of mind to leave her again. Suddenly headlights illuminated the area as a vehicle drove in to the car park. The girl shrank back to merge further into the tree shadows, but it was only a lone man who went into the gents and left quickly. Ten minutes later a pale coloured Honda turned in. The girl held her breath as a woman and a man got out. The man opened the boot and released two lively spaniels barking in anticipation of their early morning walk. After a few moments of coat shrugging and glove pulling they walked off briskly towards the woodland track. Then the woman changed her mind and jogged back to the toilets. She was out again in seconds with the blanketed bundle in her arms shouting urgently for the man who had wandered on with the dogs. Alerted to the emergency he reappeared quickly and the girl watched as he jabbed hurriedly at his mobile phone. The woman got into the car nursing the baby close, protecting the tiny head with the practised care of an experienced mother As the spectacle unfolded in front of her the girl's tears began to fall. They streamed down her face noiselessly in an unstoppable torrent. She felt the warm blood heavy between her legs escape the sodden padding and start to trickle down her thighs as her whole body became consumed with the throbbing and sobbing of her loss.

A police vehicle and ambulance appeared in flashing convoy and within minutes they were screaming down the road followed by the Honda.

'Bye-bye my Tingalay-o,' whispered the inconsolable girl softly as she turned away.

Life resumed. The girl's body recovered quickly. She held her avid breath as the news of an abandoned baby broke, spread and passed. The trauma left a gaping abyss in her body which filled with misgiving, guilt, self-loathing and longing. She looked in the mirror and was surprised to see herself outwardly unchanged when inside she knew nothing would ever be the same again. Over and over she replayed her actions. The logic of her plan, so understandable in the terror of her situation now seemed incomprehensible. How could she have believed that she would put it behind her without enormous emotional consequences? She had miscalculated the attachment she would feel for her child, the overwhelming passion she was unable to control. The pregnancy had been a finite event. Now the aftermath was infinite.

More than once the girl wondered if it would be better to come clean but the motivations for her original actions remained the reasons for never telling. She thought about her parents, the sacrifices they made every day and how proud they were of her academic success. In their difficult lives she was their shining example of achievement against the odds and a role model for her younger siblings. A place at a prestigious university for their daughter was beyond the wildest imaginings of immigrants who had arrived from Jamaica with nothing. Success for their children was their only aspiration, a return for their own relentless hard work and endurance. She could not let one fumbled, ill-judged and alcohol-fuelled episode wreck that reward. Of the father she thought not at all. Their mutual morning-after embarrassment and careful avoidance since said it all. He knew nothing about her too belatedly acknowledged pregnancy. The solitary secret was hers alone. Now the time for admission was passed. Her duplicity would only be a calamity heaped upon a disaster.

The pressure built as examinations approached. The girl submerged herself in study, determined that her wretched actions should not be for nothing. She worked herself into a frenzy of revision trying to frustrate the only thing her mind wanted to focus on, where it journeyed to instinctively at every unguarded minute of every day. Her final examination was an English paper. She wrote feverishly and, as the papers were collected she sat in silence, diminished by the intensity of her effort. Through the large hall windows she watched a single grey raincloud drift out of nowhere. As vestiges of light seeping from the obscured sun frilled its edges and an unseasonal silvery drizzle started to fall she laid her head on the desk and wept.

The Tightrope Walker

On 23rd June 2013 Nik Wallenda crossed the Little Colorado River Gorge in the Grand Canyon on a high wire.

My life is more treacherous than his. Every day I walk my own tightrope.

Dan leaves the house early, by quarter to eight at the latest, and I'm left giving the girls their breakfast, helping them find their PE kit, their library books, their tuck money. I've told them to pack their bags the night before.

'All set for tomorrow?' I ask.

'Yes, Mummy,' says Molly, and she usually is. Katya stares and stomps out of the room. At nine and three quarters, and ten and a half, they should be old enough to be responsible for some things in their lives. Surely.

And so I go on, footstep by footstep.

'Fiona.' That's what Dan's daughter calls me on a good day. 'Molly's hidden my homework.'

Molly freezes. Her lip trembles. 'No, I haven't.'

'Where is it then?' Katya narrows her eyes.

'I don't know.'

I can see where this is going. Molly's going to cry, I'll cuddle her, and Katya will accuse me of siding with her again.

I sigh. It's no use asking why the homework isn't in the bag already, but I do it anyway.

'Why are you always picking on me?' shouts Katya.

On the outside I am calm. 'Go and look for your book.'

'You're not my mother. You can't tell me what to do.'

'I am the adult in charge of you at the moment,' I reply firmly. 'So go and look for your book.'

'Right,' says Katya as she clumps away up the stairs, 'I'm telling Dad you wouldn't help me.'

Molly starts crying, and the whole morning charade is underway in only a slightly different form from yesterday.

On the way to school, I can see Katya's lower lip jutting forward in the mirror, her face dark with anger, and I can hear Molly snivelling. I try to smile equally at both of them at the gate. I give Molly a hug. Katya pulls away from me, glowering.

'See you later, girls.' Tears prick my eyes.

Katya runs off and I see her bump into another child on purpose. Molly clings to my hand.

'I don't like Katya. I wish we didn't have to live with them.'

'You like Dan, don't you?'

Molly nods.

'It's early days, love.'

'It's been since January, Mummy. That's six months.' Molly's crying again. 'I don't like Katya. She's horrible.'

The whistle blows, and Molly lets go of me.

Every day my tightrope wobbles, and I daren't look beyond the next step.

When Nik Wallenda crossed the Little Colorado River Gorge, he had no safety harness. Nik's walk was on a two-inch thick steel cable, 1,500 feet in the air. The quarter of a mile took him 22 minutes.

I have no idea how long my tightrope is, just that every step is treacherous. In my lunch break I sit in the café with a jacket potato, and try to see a way to improve the lives of the two people I love most in the world, Dan and Molly, and one feisty ten year old I planned to win round with kindness and love. I'd thought it would be easy. How foolish I'd been.

I chew coleslaw absent-mindedly. Dan is a kind and lovely person. He says the divorce was messy; he says Katya's mother has moved to a new life three hundred miles away. She didn't want to take Katya with her.

I'd met Dan's daughter lots of times of course, mostly when Molly was off with her dad for the weekend. Katya's the sort of girl who'd rather be climbing a tree or bouncing on a trampoline, than playing Scrabble or Othello, things Molly likes to do. She was always very polite when Dan and I took her out. It was only when we told her about our plan to live together that she started to change. Or perhaps she was like it anyway, and I simply couldn't see beyond the face of the man I love.

'She's becoming a teenager a bit early,' Dan said. 'She's a good kid.'

As far as I can tell, she isn't anything like a good kid. As Molly said this morning, she's horrible.

I look round the café guiltily. I am appalled that I've had that thought. What makes it worse is that whenever I try and talk to Dan about Katya, he sides with her, he really does. And I suppose I always side with Molly.

I start the afternoon with only half my mind on my job, recording the state of people's teeth, suctioning a patient's mouth, passing the dentist sterile tools. It doesn't seem fair: Dan and I have a chance of happiness together, and that child is doing everything she can to spoil it.

'She'll get used to you,' Dan says.

Once, when things were really bad for me and Molly, he looked sadly at me.

'This isn't working, is it?'

And then he said he was sorry, it was probably his fault. He had so much marking to do, so much lesson preparation, perhaps he hadn't been fair in asking me to come and share his life.

I think about the tightrope walker, Nik Wallenda. He came from a long line of circus performers. Tightrope walking was in his genes. His mother made him a pair of elk-skin soled shoes to keep a grip on the cable as he took step after step. And not only that, he was murmuring prayers almost constantly along the way.

I haven't prayed for a long time. I don't think I believe in prayer any more. I look out of the window in between patients, speak silently to a god I don't believe in. Nothing remarkable happens. A bus goes past in the street below, the hygienist pops in to speak to the dentist.

I've started to dread going home in the evening. Perhaps I was expecting too much. Maybe I should listen to Molly, pack our bags and leave. Step off the tightrope, move back into life before Dan.

I pick up the girls from their after school club. Katya's sitting on a chair holding her arm. She looks paler than usual.

'Are you OK, love?'

She starts crying.

'Hey, what is it? Do you feel poorly?'

'She had a fight with someone at break,' says the carer. 'She's in big trouble. There's a letter for her father in her bag.'

'I've been suspended.' She speaks without emotion.

The tightrope seems to sway beneath my feet.

'I'd better get you home.' What else can I say?

In the car, Molly breaks the silence. She's keen to tell me about the story she's written. Her teacher says it's her best one ever.

'Creep,' says Katya, and Molly stops.

'I'll tell you later, Mummy,' she whispers, and I know she's almost crying again.

Katya's still clutching her arm as we walk into the house.

'You'd better let me have a look at that.' I say.

'I'm showing Dad,' she says.

I pour glasses of squash for the girls. I suggest Molly might like to watch a video, while I talk to Katya.

'Well done about the story,' I say. 'I'm very proud of you.'

'Nobody's proud of me,' says Katya.

'I think we should talk. Off you go, Molly.'

'I want Dad,' says Katya.

'Look love, your Dad's not going to be home for a while, so why don't you try talking to me. Maybe I can help.'

'You can't. Besides, you're not my mother.'

'I wish I was,' I say, 'then you'd let me help, wouldn't you?'

She stares at me. She hasn't seen her mother since she left the city. No wonder the poor kid's angry. Every day she sees me with Molly, the two of us talking like friends. We are friends. Every other weekend she watches as Molly goes off with her father, a man she trusts, a man who loves her.

Like me, Katya's on a tightrope. One parent's gone. Who's to say the other won't get fed up with her, push her out of his life? Though I know Dan won't do that, and surely Katya must know too.

Katya picks up her drink and I follow her up the stairs with my mug of tea. There's a small sofa in her room, where her friends can sit. Only they haven't been for a while. Maybe they're fed up with someone who pushes people for nothing, someone who picks fights, someone who is angry all the time.

'I don't want you in my room,' she says.

'I want to help.'

'You can't.' Katya bangs her door in my face.

Downstairs I chop vegetables viciously, stir onions forcefully round the pan. What right had I to bring my daughter into this house, into this atmosphere which is destroying us? My tightrope wobbles dangerously. I haven't got Nik Wallenda's strength of character. I've had enough. I want to pack my bag, take Molly's hand, and go.

Dan comes home, comments on the delicious smell, sees my face, holds me. I tell him about Katya, that she's in trouble at school; that I wanted to help, and she wouldn't talk to me.

Dan goes upstairs, knocks at Katya's door. He's with her for a long time. Molly asks me if it's nearly dinner time, and I hug her and say, 'Not quite.' We both hear Dan come out of Katya's bedroom. I'll tell him this evening that I think it'd be better if Molly and I leave.

I hear Katya shouting from the top of the stairs.

'No I will not. She's not my mother.'

I stand by the kitchen door, holding on to Molly's shoulder. Dan's footsteps stop. His voice is quiet, controlled.

'No, thank God,' he says.

I think of Nik Wallenda, whose mother made him a pair of elk-skin shoes to keep a grip on the cable as he moved. He would have fallen off but for her thoughtfulness, her faith in him, her courage.

'Your mother abandoned you, Kat. She doesn't want to see you ever again. Fiona is prepared to love you, if you will only give her a chance.'

'You're hurting me, Mummy.'

I let go of Molly's shoulder.

Dan thumps the banister. 'And if you start being nice to Molly, she might let you be her sister.'

He comes downstairs, white-faced.

Katya's very quiet during dinner. She keeps looking at her father, but he can't or won't meet her eyes. She seems small, broken almost, a child who doesn't know how to make her pain go away. She'll be better off by far if Molly and I disappear out of her life.

At bed-time, I sit on Molly's bed and we talk. It's like old times. I go into the room I share with Dan, lift my suitcase from the top of the wardrobe, begin to pack some of my clothes.

'What are you doing?' Dan's running his hand through his hair.

'It's no good, Dan. She'll never accept me, and her behaviour's getting worse.'

He stares at me for a moment. I want him to argue, to try and persuade me to stay, but he doesn't.

He knows it's for the best then.

My tightrope's wobbling badly now. I wish I had the equivalent of those elk-skin shoes. I wish I was somebody else, anyone except me.

I fill my case, close the lid, pull the zip slowly round it.

There's a tug at my sleeve. I turn, expecting Molly. It's Katya. She looks very young in her pink nightie. She's holding a teddy bear. Her face is blotchy, her eyes red.

She hesitates, throws herself into my arms, weeping. We are both weeping.

'Don't go, Fiona.'

The wire still wobbles as Nik Wallenda steps towards dry land.

Authors in Residence

Jeremy Turner, proprietor of a North London bookshop, The Page Turner, closed the door and turned towards Holly, his assistant.

'That went well, don't you think?' he said. 'Although we're lucky that book didn't land a few inches closer to the shelf. That really was a narrow escape.'

Holly exhaled. 'I'll say.'

The evening at Jeremy's shop – featuring a reading by a popular local author – had attracted about 100 people who were invited to browse the shelves during an interval. As the audience settled for the second half, there was a commotion. A book, the *Oxford Companion to English Literature* – a heavyweight tome in every respect – tumbled from the top shelf and narrowly avoided landing directly on the woman sitting underneath. It brushed her shoulder and fell to the floor with a loud crash. The woman, though shaken, stayed for the remainder of the reading before leaving in the company of four people who were sitting close to her. They said they would take her to A&E just as a precaution.

'The next time we stage one of these evenings, we'll remove books from the top shelves,' Jeremy said as he crossed to the scene of the incident. 'Did you think there was something strange about the people that woman left with? I could've sworn they weren't here for the first half and their clothes were odd too.'

'I didn't really notice. I was just glad she was OK,' Holly said as she picked up the *Oxford Companion to English Literature*, now repositioned on to a lower shelf. 'My God, this could've caused real damage. It weighs a ton.'

She leafed through the book and frowned. 'There's something odd here. Blank pages, no, not pages, blank columns...no text where there should be some.'

She passed the book to Jeremy who nodded.

'I see what you mean. Now, why would that be? It almost looks as if the entries for some authors have been deleted. The first entry under K is blank, there's a gap between Orton and Osborne, a space in the A section and another under H.

Bizarre. I'll order a replacement copy tomorrow. OK, time to close up...it's been a long day.'

Tom Powell ran his hands through his thinning hair. *My hair is thinning and I'm still only 29,* he thought. *This job is truly getting to me.* It wasn't just the hours – although they were bad enough – but also the nature of the job. It seemed an unwritten rule that junior doctors on the A&E ward of the North London hospital were assigned a disproportionate number of night shifts and Tom, recently qualified, was on his third such slot that week.

'Crackpots, cracked heads and crack addicts' was his laconic description of a typical evening's intake of A&E patients; tonight had been no exception. He looked up as the triage nurse poked her head around the door.

'Got a minute, Dr Powell?' she asked.

'Of course, come in.'

'I just wanted to mark your card,' the nurse said. 'We have a group of new admissions out here who seem a bit odd.'

'Odd? As opposed to the well-adjusted citizens I've dealt with so far this evening? That guy with second degree burns who'd been slammed into the doner-kebab thingy after an argument, for instance...odder than that?'

'A different type of odd, more refined.' She opened the door. 'Dr Powell, this is Mrs Gladys Carpenter.'

Tom watched as a lady shuffled into his office. She seemed embarrassed by the attention and explained that she'd been struck by an object and persuaded to attend A&E although she was sure no serious injury had been inflicted.

'OK, Mrs Carpenter, it's my job to make sure about that. Now, what was the object?'

'The *Oxford Companion to English Literature*, Doctor.'

Oh God, Tom thought, *another crackpot.*

'I see,' he replied. 'And how exactly did this happen?'

As she told Tom about the incident in The Page Turner, fatigue coursed through him and his placid temperament began to crumble...this was a waste of his time, a waste of her time and a waste of NHS resources. He curtly asked her how many fingers he'd raised; she answered correctly and added that she didn't feel dizzy.

'Well, Mrs Carpenter, it's probably nothing worse than a split infinitive or perhaps a dangling participle,' he drawled, ushering her out of the room. 'Nurse! Next, please.'

The nurse re-appeared with a middle-aged man who wore a shabby serge jacket over his V-necked jumper, shirt and tie. He had an assessing gaze and sported a thin moustache which seemed to cling to his upper lip. The nurse announced: 'Mr Eric Blair.'

The newcomer smiled and said, 'Call me George, everybody else does.' He said that he'd been resting contentedly until a fall jolted him awake. He felt disorientated and thought it best to see a doctor. Reluctant to impart more information, George cast an anxious glance towards Tom's computer screen and the various pieces of equipment in the surgery.

'Why are there so many cameras in the hospital and on the streets?'

Another crackpot...and, worse, a paranoid one, Tom thought as he explained about the CCTV cameras. George leaned back and mumbled, 'I thought as much – a police state.'

Tom asked whether George wished to be referred to a consultant for a further check. George shuddered and waved his hand.

'No, they've got enough on me already. They're not getting anything else,' he said and left.

With trepidation, Tom asked for the next patient and a dark-haired woman, wearing a high-necked gown and a pearl necklace, edged into the room. She clutched a bonnet and bag and smiled shyly.

'Come in...take a seat, Miss er...'

'It's Miss Austen, Doctor. I came over quite faint and was advised to visit you.'

Tom heard that she had been resting and woke to experience a falling sensation – much like George, thought Tom – and found herself in a bookshop or a book emporium, as she called it. 'I have a great interest in literature so I perused the books and purchased one. It's a scandalous book which any young lady could hardly be expected to understand but when I saw that the author – E.L. James – was female, I felt quite faint.'

Tom rolled his eyes and asked her to slip off her gown so that he could check her heartbeat. Miss Austen seemed about to swoon but rallied and murmured, 'Oh, Doctor, must I really?'

A few minutes later, Tom dismissed her, saying that she was perfectly well.

Miss Austen joined her three companions in the waiting room. Setting aside the book she had been reading, she flicked through some magazines which were on a table. She then rummaged in her bag and produced a small bamboo and lace fan which she wafted delicately in front of her face.

Another of the group, Franz, a man with sharp facial features and haunted eyes, became embroiled in a discussion with a girl on the admissions desk.

'As I said, I can't do anything until you confirm your identity,' the girl said.

'I do not have my papers with me,' Franz replied.

'In which case, I'll refer you to my colleague upstairs. First, you must fill out this form.'

'But it requires some form of identification and I do not have...'

'Yes, you don't have your papers – we've established that,' the girl said. 'OK, you must complete this form to receive a temporary visitor card.'

'Why? I am not a temporary anything. I merely wish to receive medical attention,' Franz replied, raising his voice and leaning towards the girl.

'Mr Kafka, please calm down or I will have to call security.'

'It is typical,' Franz said, turning towards the others. 'Layers of bureaucracy and then they threaten to arrest me even though I have done nothing wrong. It was similar when we boarded the bus earlier. The world is just as I described in my writings.'

Miss Austen grimaced. Earlier, Franz had been irate when told that he required either an Oyster card or the precise fare before boarding the bus. He railed against 'authoritarian red tape' and an unfortunate scene was only averted when Mrs Carpenter offered to pay his fare with a £10 note; one which Miss Austen examined. *How nice it would be to be portrayed on that note*, she thought, aware that a woman was unlikely to ever do so. She felt a nudge of her shoulder; it was the fourth member of the group – a twinkly-eyed man with a white beard protruding over the rolled neck of his thick cable-knit jumper. He nodded towards Franz: 'Do you know that asshole?'

Miss Austen blushed. 'I'm afraid not, sir. I may have misheard his name but it sounded like Cavendish. Perhaps he's one of the Cavendish's of Eaton Square.'

'Don't think so, lady, he ain't no Brit. Puny little guy, looks like an insect.'

'Oh my days,' sighed Miss Austen. 'I feel that is harsh, Mr...I'm afraid I didn't catch your name.'

'Ernest, but call me Papa.' He picked up a newspaper from the table. 'How about that? My buddy Fidel is still alive and well. Now, that calls for one of Cuba's finest.'

Papa produced a huge cigar and lit it. A siren sounded and, seconds later, two security guards rushed into the room, grabbed him roughly and only loosened their grip when the cigar had been extinguished and confiscated. They departed as another door opened and a dishevelled man staggered into the room. He advanced towards the TV screen positioned high up on the wall.

'Nurse!' he bellowed. 'Can ya change that to a different channel? I hate, feckin' hate, that reality TV stuff.'

The nurse glared at him. 'Be quiet, Michael. You're drunk – again – and I'm not changing the channel. It's my favourite programme; I love Big Brother.'

George shook his head as he said to the others: 'Just like I wrote...surveillance cameras everywhere, down-and-outs on the streets, people saying they love Big Brother. Britain *has* become a police state.'

'I think the world remains as I envisaged it. Look at these magazines.' Miss Austen said as she pointed to a headline: *Boy-band heart-throb Gary shows us his new dream home and says: "All I want now is someone to share it with."'*

She looked up and said, 'It is a truth universally acknowledged, that a single man in possession of a good fortune must be in want of a wife. Some things have changed since my day; in that E.L. James book, the couple have dispensed with chaperones, dance cards, a proper period of courtship and they have a fondness for whips and chains which I find unfathomable but it is, in essence, a young woman falling for the charms of a handsome, wealthy man. *Plus ça change,* as the French say.'

'Aww, bullshit...it ain't like I wrote,' Papa snorted, jerking a scarred thumb towards the newspaper. 'This world's full of lily-livered wimps. Hunting is banned, bull-fighting is frowned on, smoking isn't allowed, wars are fought by launching unmanned vehicles as missiles, there's no hand-to-hand combat and people run to a hospital with the merest graze of their shoulder. You ask me, there's only one real man left.'

He turned the newspaper to a page which showed a muscular, toned Vladimir Putin, stripped to the waist. 'There, that guy; apparently, he wrestles bears when he's not running his country and he's a goddamn Russian. I want to return to the comfort of that book. I was happier there, I think you lot were too.'

George nodded. 'I agree. Let's get the omnibus back to that nice bookshop and our places in literary history. This world isn't for us.'

Franz and Miss Austen rose to their feet and followed Papa and George out of the room.

Expression

I gave up speaking a month ago. Funny thing, it took at least two days for anyone to notice. Blah, blah, blah. People open their months and crap pours out. No one bothers to listen, not really. They just wait their turn to churn out their own crap. Even teachers bark out instructions but don't listen.

Everyone's always telling me not to do things they do: don't smoke, don't drink, don't cross the road until the green man appears; or to do things they don't – fasten your back seat belt, eat healthily, exercise, blah, blah, blah.

I want to speak words worth hearing.

'Well.' Doctor Haines lowers her hands from my jaw and turns to Mum. 'As far as I can tell, there's nothing physically wrong. When did you say it started?'

'The beginning of this month,' Mum repeats. She watches me in the way she does Dad when he's had one too many.

'Is there anything which could have triggered emotional trauma?'

Mum's lips mould into their habitual slump. 'No, like I said, nothing out of the ordinary...'

'Mm,' Haines pronounces.

A favourite of doctors: 'mm'. Means they don't have a clue, but they'll not admit it – not to the likes of me or Mum.

'I think the best route for Phoebe would be a psychiatric evaluation.'

Phoebe – stupid name. Mum was into episodes of *Friends* when pregnant with me. Now I'm laden with a name more suited to a dog.

'A shrink?' Mum says.

'A psychiatrist.' Haines speaks as if Mum is younger than her. 'There's no stigma to these problems any more, Mrs Yard.'

But 'these problems' have stigma built into their slip around words.

Haines turns to me. 'What do you think, about that Phoebe?'

I shrug. I want to get away from the smell of disinfectant hand-wash, and next door's patient, hacking up his lungs.

Mum gives her a look as if to say, 'you won't catch her out that easily'. Instead, she says, 'I should speak to her father first...'

'Does Phoebe's father live with you?'

Mum's down-turned lips crumple to a rotten rosebud formation.

'You understand I have to ask, Mrs Yard. Family life is very...diverse nowadays.'

Diverse equals crap.

'Of course.' Mum rolls the hem of her skirt and looks like a child herself. 'I'm afraid he'll be anti that type of treatment.'

'I'll tell you what I'll do, Mrs Yard. I'll book an appointment – it'll be a few months before Phoebe gets seen. Let's see how things go. If her condition remains, I'd recommend you attend. In the meantime, you can discuss it with your husband.'

Mum's lips move as if she wants to reply but nothing comes out.

On the bus ride home, Mum doesn't speak. She sits upright, hugging her grocery sack, lips pinched, and her hair dragged back. She looks as if every muscle and joint has frozen, except her mouth; her lips move as if rehearsing words will help her place something back into perspective. She stares out of the window, not focusing on the boarded shop fronts and graffiti-splattered walls. But her head turns as we pass the pub and her lips form wider shapes one after the other, without sound.

We fight our way past bikes in the hall and Mum unlocks our front door. There's a smell of day-old curry and frying pan oil. Once inside, she asks if I want a juice. I shake my head and slouch at the kitchen table, picking at the plastic stripping whilst she puts on the kettle and pulls a chipped and faded mug from the cupboard. She dunks her teabag, squashing it against the side of a smug Garfield. I used to love Garfield until Tammy Hill cornered me in the playground and bit the head off my rubber. When I cried, she said she knew Garfield was for babies.

Mum rings Gran. 'Hi, how are you? Fine, we're fine. Thought you'd want to know how it went. No, no need. Of course I will. Yes, okay. No, really. There's been no trouble. Please, don't start...Phoebe's fine. No, what's the point?'

Mum rolls her eyes. 'She won't talk to you – it's not personal, don't take it like that. The doctor said to give it time. Yes, that's all. No. Yes, we'll come and visit soon, promise. Yes, you too. Bye.'

Frowning, Mum sits next to me; she brushes my fringe aside.

'Who can I talk to?' she says, and looks off out of the window.

Talk to me. Say something other than, 'eat your greens, do your homework, tuck your shirt in, don't mind your father'. Smile. Please smile.

She sighs. 'You need to get your fringe trimmed.' Now she looks at me. 'Phoebe love, where are you going? Don't run off. You wanna watch TV?'

I can't slam the door 'cause it sticks. I stomp up the stairs louder than I'd dare if he was home.

They kick off as soon as he gets in. Dad's voice is loud and slurred. Mum apologises, says dinner wouldn't keep. I wish the neighbours had their TV at its usual level. I bury my head under my pillow and hum. His words stop making sense. Mum yells and it's followed by a thud. My breathing quickens until it hurts in my chest. I listen harder. I can't move. He mumbles apologies and her reassurance is faint but audible. At least I can breathe again.

It's dark when he leaves in the morning. Grey light filters through the curtains and the ring of damp on the wallpaper grows visible.

I rub my nose and blow into the air, watching my breath mushroom to life. It starts to evaporate, and I make a dash for it. Once in the bathroom at the sink, I throw a towel on the floor and stand on it. I twist the tap and squeeze toothpaste onto my brush. I scrub. When I'm done I run the hot tap and lukewarm water thaws my fingers. I breathe on the mirror and draw a smiley face. Mum knocks on the door and asks me how much longer I'll be. I wipe the glass clear.

'Morning Phoebe,' she tries, as we pass in the hall. Her voice is strained bright; her hair's in a tangle, the corner of her eye is darkening. 'Your father was late in last night,' she says as if it's unusual. 'I hope we didn't wake you.'

I shrug.

'You finished in the bathroom?'

I nod.

'I'll just be a minute, then I'll fix us some toast.'

She locks the door behind her.

She'll have foundation in her dressing gown pocket.

She's on the morning shift at the hospital, collecting trays and washing out water jugs plus a bit of damp dusting. She'll offer to walk with me to the school gates, but if Tammy sees, it'll be worse for me.

At lunchtime, I take refuge in the sports hall.

But Tammy finds me, nicks my *Wotsits,* and stamps on my sandwiches.

'Hey, mutey. You got anything to say, today?' She pushes her face into mine, powdered cheese taints her breath. Her two backups lurk behind her.

'Your dad's a wino loser,' she says. Her voice echoes, it's as if the walls are in collaboration with her.

I'm pressed against a gymnasium railing. I half turn away from her.

'Hey, look at me, mutey. You must have somethin' to say, cat gotcha tongue?'

I look through the side window and pretend she's not there.

'How's Miss Mop?'

My shoulders bunch up, cramming my neck. This is a new tack for Tammy. She calls me a baby if she sees Mum walking me to school, but her insults are reserved for me and him.

'Your mum's a miserable witch...'

I swing at her, fist knuckle-tight. I feel the crunch of her nose. One of the backups sidles off.

Tammy cradles her face, blood seeps between her fingers.

'What have you done?' The other backup gulps, mouth unhinged like a broken puppet.

'You're a bloody freak,' she says, but steps back from me. 'I'll get a teacher.'

Tammy nods and moans.

I want to run, but my legs won't budge.

When Mr Bradley arrives, they say I attacked Tammy for no reason. He tells me to wait outside his room.

After an hour he gives up with, 'you've got to apologise'. He finishes on a lecture about the evils of violence, and promises that my parents will be informed.

I pull on my jeans and a baggy top and head for the kitchen. Mum fusses with bread under the grill. Dad flicks through the post. He jabs his thumb beneath an envelope seal and rips, leaving a jagged mess.

'Morning, Phoebe,' Mum says, voice high and bright.

He points at me, shaking a chunky finger into my face. 'You'd better start talking today missy – I'm not putting up with any more of your nonsense.'

He unfolds the letter and reads it. The muscle in his jaw starts to twitch. Mum turns back to the grill her mouth shaping voiceless words.

'What the hell is this? You're not sending my daughter to a shrink.'

'It's not my idea,' Mum says.

'Bloody ridiculous. I'll bet this was your mother's doing. Tell her to stop interfering. When were you going to tell me?'

Mum turns the bread but it's started to blacken.

'It wasn't anything to do with Mum. The doctor thought it'd be for the best.'

'Bloody doctors, what do they know?' He wrenches back his chair and lurches around the table, breathing hard and staring at me. 'You say something, Phoebe, or I'll make you.'

'Paul!' Mum jerks the pan out and turns. 'Leave her alone, please.'

'Pleeease. We've already one mouse in this household.' He grabs a handful of my hair and yanks it towards him. I clench my teeth against the pain. He pulls me closer still. I can smell the bitterness of day-old beer. He never gets this close to me – not in affection, not in anger.

'You speak!' he says.

I hum instead. Hum and hum to blot him out.

He frowns and shakes my shoulder. 'Shut up!'

I hum louder.

'Stop!' Mum smacks the pan on the table. He releases me and turns to her.

The pan slips from her hands and clatters onto the floor.

'Go,' she says.

It'll be worse for us both if I stay. My heart works faster than my legs. I dive under my blankets. I hear her yell and the thud. The front door slams.

Silence.

I can't move.

After a few minutes, the sound of footsteps and a tap on my door. 'Phoebe, love,' Mum says. 'You all right?'

Her face is red and puffy. She places a hand over her mouth as if to plug up a sob. She says, 'Put a few things – essential things in your school bag.'

I have questions, but can't form the words. I gather uniform: shirts and skirts, favourite jeans and top; my pencil case and diary. I leave my Garfield mug – he's the only one who ever grins around here.

Once on the bus, Mum takes my hand and squeezes.

'We're going to stay at Gran's,' she says. 'I know I said I wouldn't, but that was before...' Her sentence fades.

In a blur, we pass the pub and graffiti-splattered walls.

I glance at Mum. Her chin trembles. She doesn't speak.

I take a breath. 'Let's not ever go back,' I say.

She turns to me, her eyes bright and filled with tears but I swear the corners of her lips relax. She brings me to her and hugs so hard. She nods and her chin brushes the top of my head.

These are the words I've held in my heart, the only ones worth hearing, and I hope they'll evoke the shape of her smile.

The Windswept Cherry Tree

In my youth, not long after the battle of Sekigahara, I sought refuge in the peace and tranquillity of the Sekita Mountains. There I came across the idyllic village of Sakurinkou, nestled in a high wooded valley. No other village could boast of such an approach. Three ornate wooden bridges crossed three rugged mountain streams then around a jut of rock emerged an avenue of blossoming cherry trees.

My heart warms at the mere memory. I can still feel, now, the soft dirt of the warn path underfoot, still smell the floral, earthy scent and feel the sharp yet refreshing mountain breeze.

The wind through the trees, rose and fell like the sea against the shore and whistled through narrow rock gullies like the sweetest flute. My weary heart felt stilled before even reaching the village proper. A dozen elegant wooden structures gripped the steep valley edge while the only flat ground lay dominated by a temple structure, its tower a full three floors high, standing defiant against the strong mountain winds. I knew then I had found my sanctuary.

Legs weary from travel, I settled myself in the village tea-house, cup in hand, and there I saw the village's only blemish, the split and corroded remains of a long dead tree. Curiously, rather than being removed or shrouded from view, it had been enshrined with grass rope and surrounded with offerings. Such reverence signified a worthy tale.

Hearing the bustling of the aged proprietor behind me, I turned. 'Honoured sir, might I enquire as to the meaning behind that stump?'

The man's wrinkles deepened as he smiled and moved forward. 'Ah, the sacred cherry tree of love.'

His expression turned dreamy as he gazed upon it.

'Many a villager found love praying beneath that tree. I, too, found my beloved wife after kneeling to it in prayer. Such a sad tale there is in its downfall. For over a hundred years the tree showered the village and all who visited with love until...'

Hashin Sou the samurai beheld the village before him. This was his place of birth and yet not even a shadowy memory remained. But deep in his soul he felt the connection; the fulfilment of homecoming. He would set up a dojo here. It was remote but, by his reputation, students would come. He would settle, find love and raise a family.

In the months following his arrival, his dojo took off, as expected. More than two dozen students sought his instruction. Yet romance eluded him. He was young no more. Few women in the village were unattached and of the young ones that were, who would look for a battle scarred, age worn, samurai as a partner? His spirits fell.

Hashin Sou prayed every day for months at the temple yet still found no love. Finally, he approached a priest in despair.

'Tell me how I might find love,' he implored. 'Daily I pray to the gods but they do not hear.'

The kindly old priest laid a hand on the samurai's shoulder.

'You have been praying in the wrong place. Try the sacred cherry tree, where the young seek their love.'

The Samurai's gaze followed the priest's hand towards the ancient form of a cherry tree. It stood, stripped bare by winter, desolate and frail against the howling wind. He had seen it before and marvelled at its grandeur but would it really bring him love?

'Pray to it every morning and when its bloom is full, love will find you.'

Despite a little doubt, the samurai followed the priest's directions in earnest, and as the tree began to bud, his spirits rose. But when bloom after bloom opened and still no love was presented, his heart fell.

Then, one morning, as he approached the cherry to pray, he saw her; a woman with hair the colour of the earth and skin as pale and fair as any Geisha. He could draw no breath and stood enraptured as the wind lifted her hair, trailing it through the air. Her beauty came not with youth but age as she could not have been many years shy of him.

She had bowed to him before he remembered his manners and, in haste, he responded with his own.

She smiled at him. 'Have you come to pray for love, too?'

Those green eyes, so rare and so alive, like the first foliage of spring. He could only nod.

'Then let us pray together.' She invited him with a gesture to kneel beside her.

All his prayers and all his wishes...

Every morning he returned and every morning she was there. They spoke, shared tea on the rise overlooking the tree and, finally, as the bloom faded, Hashin Sou declared his love and asked for her hand in marriage.

'I can think of no greater honour.' She held out her hand. 'But know this; I have no family that can vouch for me or pay my way. I am alone in this world.'

Hashin Sou had long been a wealthy and independent man. He needed no dowry or family connections to dictate his love and so they were wed. Before that very cherry tree they gave their vows. Years of happy union followed and the birth of two fine children, a boy and a girl. But such happiness was never meant for mortals and so one windswept night it ended.

That night the samurai was woken by the fiercest howling wind he could ever recall. The very timbers creaked around them and his wife sat huddled against her knees with such fear tightening her face.

Hashin Sou drew his wife into his arms and held her tight.

'The house is strong. There is nothing to fear.'

But she shook her head, tears flowing down her cheeks.

'I cannot withstand it. It tears at my limbs. I cannot...'

'Do not fear...' the samurai calmed her. 'There is no wind in here.'

But her fear did not ease.

'I am sorry.' She turned her tear streaked face towards him. 'You prayed so diligently to me and yet I could find no mortal to share your love and so I sought to share it myself. But our time is at an end. I can feel my body breaking. Please, show your love to me through our children. They will stay with you even if I cannot.'

She... She couldn't be... Hashin Sou's gaze passed through the wall in the direction of the cherry. He had fallen in love with the spirit of the cherry tree.

As his mind searched for a way to save the tree, the crack

of breaking timber sounded, louder even than the wind, and he turned to his wife in horror. All he could do was gaze into her green eyes as they faded away into nothing.

As soon as dawn broke and the wind died, Hashin Sou dashed out to the remains of the cherry tree, his beautiful wife. Her trunk had been completely severed with only a jagged stump left in place.

As he knelt, his hand on her bark, in an agonised silence, the children emerged. Solemnly, they approached the crushed canopy of their fallen mother and each took four twigs. These they planted on either side of the path leading to the village so the seeds of their mother's beauty could live on. And so they have, to this day.

Having stared fixedly at the stump throughout the tale, I finally turned my gaze. The sorrow of the tale left my soul heavy.

'And what of the samurai?'

The old man refilled my cup.

'He could no longer find the energy to train himself or others and so gave up the way of the samurai. He sat here on this very slope every day, keeping watch over the remains of his wife. Eventually, he built a house here, so he could see her every moment and, in time, he started serving tea to travellers.'

'Then you are...?' My grip slipped on the cup in my hand, spilling tea across the table.

The old man nodded.

'If you wish to see my wife in all her glory, return here just before midnight.'

It seemed an odd instruction and, I reasoned, the old man could have made the whole story up. Still, the haunting tale would not leave my mind and I tossed in my bed that night until just before midnight when I rose. There was no harm in looking. I was awake, anyway.

I returned to the stump and found the old man waiting there. A man and a woman, not much older than me, stood at each side of him. Their eyes! Even in the moonlight, the rare green could not be mistaken. Could the tale be true?

'She comes!' The woman pointed into air above the stump.

I gasped. From nothing, burst the form of a majestic cherry tree in full bloom, not substantial but as if etched in the air by the moonlight. It stayed for the briefest of moments and then vanished.

I have journeyed far since that time and never again seen such a wonder. Every spring at the first sight of the cherry blossoms, my mind returns to that quiet village and their sacred cherry tree stump. I often wonder if I ought to have stayed there, longer than the brief few months I did, and prayed to the cherry tree for love. But then I remember the tale and that love can bring both joy and sorrow, for nothing lasts forever, even the trees.

Left-overs

'Stop cryin'. Stop cryin' or I'll 'it yer.'

She didn't stop cryin', so I 'it her. She shut up then. I was worried that Dad might come back and find out we was makin' some noise. Then we'd both get 'it 'cause Dad told us we was to keep quiet in this place and Dad's got a really bad temper if people don't do what 'e says.

But Treena don't cry so much now. Before, when Dad was out, she was always snivellin' and askin' for Mum. I got fed up tellin' 'er I didn't know where she was. Now she acts different; she sucks 'er thumb most all the time and sits on the floor and kind of rocks backwards and forwards.

I know why she cried though. She's 'ungry, like me. It's gettin' colder too. I think it's October now, though I've lost count of days and stuff, but the nights are longer than before. I should've gone back to school by now and Treena should've started in Reception class. She was gonna 'ave my school sweater which'd got too tight and Mum'd got me a new one specially, but without 'er and in this new place, nothin's the same.

There's not much furniture down 'ere in this flat, but I pulled a wood chair over so I could climb up to the kitchen cupboards to 'ave another look. Whenever Dad comes back 'e always brings 'is beer and biscuits and crisps and some milk, but all the packets are empty now. Right on the top shelf I saw a couple of pizza boxes and pulled 'em down. There was a small slice left in each one. They'd gone all dry and chewy but Treena and me shared 'em. I saw the little plastic wraps of white powder at the back of another shelf, but I ain't gonna touch 'em again. Treena and me thought they might be sherbet and tried some. It was 'orrible and we both threw up afterwards.

Dad 'asn't ever stayed away so long before. Though 'e said I wasn't to leave Treena, I've been out nickin' food when we were 'ungry. I can run fast and it were easy to start with. Apples or oranges from outside the greengrocers and cakes and bread rolls from the minimarket. But they know me now and if I go near, they watch me like a 'awk – same as the big supermarket. And I daren't go too far away from this basement flat 'cause I'm scared I wouldn't find me way back and scared that Dad might come back and find me not 'ere.

The electrics went off yesterday so we can't watch the little telly anymore. There ain't no books 'ere to look at neither. I try to remember the stories Uncle Leon used to read to us and tell 'em again to Treena, but I ain't very good at it. Each day is twice as long as it used to be. We sleep a lot once it gets dark. I wish me mum were 'ere – it would be a lot nicer – we weren't never 'ungry with 'er . . .

Dad was away on that long 'oliday. I don't think Treena even remembered what 'e looked like, 'cause she was a baby when Dad left. Soon, I couldn't remember 'im very well either. I liked the school I went to, with Mum and Treena comin' to meet me at the gates each day. We'd all watch the telly together at 'ome and Mum got us lovely food with chips and things. I can't really remember when Uncle Leon started comin' round. Mum laughed a lot when 'e came and sort of looked prettier. Uncle Leon took us all out – sometimes to a cafe; sometimes to a cinema and 'e'd buy popcorn for us to take in. That 'ad never 'appened wi' Dad. And when we went to bed, Uncle Leon would read us a story. Mum ain't very good at readin', but she loved 'em stories too and would come into our bedroom, sit on my bed cuddlin' me, while Uncle Leon cuddled Treena and we'd all listen together.

Even when Mum got sick and was throwin' up in the mornin's, she still looked 'appy. So did Uncle Leon. But it all changed when that letter arrived.

Mum was 'olding it in 'er 'and when she spoke to Treena and me.

'Your Dad's – 'is – 'is 'oliday is gonna be over soon. E'll be coming back 'ere and we're all gonna have to be real nice to 'im, 'cause he 'asn't 'ad a very good time.'

I knew what Dad would enjoy.

'Maybe Uncle Leon can take 'im to the cinema with us and listen to the stories 'e tells us all at bedtime.'

'No!' Mum's voice was not like usual. It was sharp and worried and she seemed to be near to cryin'. 'Uncle Leon has to go away. You ain't to mention 'is name. D'you understand?'

She'd gripped me and Treena by an arm and it 'urt. Treena began to whimper and then Mum was cryin' too and the grips become 'ugs.

'It'll be alright. Just – just don't argue with your dad, or upset 'im at all. Better not to speak to 'im unless he asks you a question – and try to keep quiet when 'e's 'ere. 'E doesn't like too much noise.'

Dad was there and waitin' in the flat three days later when I came back from school with Mum and Treena. It'd been so long, I didn't recognise 'im and I didn't like it much when 'e came on to me, pretend boxin' and shoutin' "Ow's my boy? 'Ow's my boy?'

Treena 'id behind Mum and wouldn't come out. When Dad pulled her to 'im, she started to cry and so 'e stopped botherin' with 'er. It felt funny that night. We was all quiet like Mum had told us to be, 'specially when Mum went to the shop to get the beer Dad asked for and we was alone with 'im. When we went to bed, 'e was watchin' telly and drinkin' - which is all 'e wanted to do each day, excep' when 'e went out late with some mates that came callin'.

I was gettin' ready for school when it all 'appened. I 'eard Mum in the loo throwin' up again. Dad 'eard 'er too. 'E started bangin' on the loo door.

'What the fuck's goin' on? You come out 'ere, bitch!'

Dad was yellin' and 'is face had gone all red and angry. Mum come out and she looked scared.

'Kids! Get in your room and close the door!' She was shoutin' at us and we were scared too. Behind our door we could 'ear quite a lot. It were Dad mostly, 'cause 'e was shoutin' over Mum's voice.

'Fuckin' whore! Did yer think I'd raise another man's kid? Get out! Go to yer lover man. Go on, clear out! And don't think you'll see yer kids again. Now, fuck off, you bitch!'

I 'eard the sound of 'ard slaps and 'its and my mum scream in pain. Then our front door banged and it went quiet. I went to the window and looked down at the entrance to our flats and saw Mum run out. 'Er nose was bleedin' and one eye was red and swollen. She didn't look back or stop runnin'.

Treena and me tried to stay quiet as mice but even our breathin' seemed noisy. Then Dad opened our door. There were some plastic bags from the supermarket in 'is hands and 'e chucked them at us.

'Quick, put yer clothes in these bags – and yer toothbrushes and pyjamas. We're leavin' and goin' somewhere else to live. Only yer clothes; nothin' else. Come on, move it!'

I 'elped Treena with 'er things and pushed what I could into the bags. When 'e came to our room again, Dad 'ad filled 'is 'oldall and 'e locked the front door behind us as we left the flat together. We walked to the next corner while Dad was talkin' on his mobile. After a while a car drove up and took us to an 'ouse. It was the first of several different 'ouses we stayed at. The men there all seemed to be Dad's friends. In some places there'd be a bed Treena and me could share, in others a sofa and sometimes we'd sleep on the floor. Dad would go out with these men at night and come back – sort of excited – with fish and chips for us or a 'amburger. Then Dad brought us to this basement flat; it's got steps up to the street outside and its own outside door.

I think we came quite a while ago, but I can't remember prop'ly. Dad'd often go out at night; sometimes 'e'd stay away two nights. Then 'e'd come back 'appy and jokin' with lots of food. 'E said we wasn't to go out or to answer the door if the bell went. Just to stay very quiet. At first we liked watching telly all the time, but it got borin' after a while. I wished I could go back to school. Now I just wish Dad would come back. I'm scared; I dunno what to do.

It were dark and we was both asleep when the bell went. We stayed quiet like Dad 'ad told us to. We 'eard voices outside and the bell went again and again. Then a man shouted: 'This is the police. If there's anyone in there, open this door!'

I could just see Treena in her bed. She looked frightened, but I 'eld my finger to my lips and she nodded and did the same.

'Come on, open up!'

It were that voice again. We stayed still as still for a long time. It started to get light and I crept out of bed and took the chair to the door to look out of the peep-'ole. There weren't anyone there. First, Treena and me just whispered to each other, but after a little while, we stopped worryin' and spoke normal like. We was so 'ungry, we couldn't think much about anything else really. I'd just decided I'd risk goin' out to try and nick some food when there was a huge bang on the door. The buildin' sort of shook and then there was another bang. The wood on the door splintered and a whole lot of policemen was suddenly in the flat.

Treena was screamin' 'er 'ead off and we both ran to our bedroom and I slammed the door. It was a policewoman what opened it. She'd taken 'er police 'at off and she was smilin' at us. Through the door I could see police at the kitchen shelf with the plastic wraps. They'd got rubber gloves on and was carefully putting them into a bag. The policewoman knelt down beside us.

'Hey, don't be scared – we're here to help. We've been looking for you for a long time. We've been really worried – so has your mum. She's going to be so pleased we've found you. You see, your dad has – your dad has had a bit of an accident and he – he couldn't get back here. But one of my mates is phoning your mum right now and we're going to bring her here as soon as we can. Wow – there's nothing to eat in the kitchen, is there? I'll bet you're hungry. Let's see if I've got anything in my pocket. Oh yes, look, here's a chocolate bar!'

She broke it up and Treena took some and started eatin' it – but I couldn't eat mine 'cause suddenly I was cryin' and cryin' and I couldn't stop.

Sad Old Man

It was to be the eulogy for a valued member of the book community. That's how they put it, and so they asked me to say something about the bookseller at his funeral because I'd known him the longest. It's true enough, but most of what I wanted to say wasn't very flattering, and I didn't think that was what they wanted to hear. I thought I'd talk to some of them and see what they said about him, which might put a different spin on things. After all, a mere employee – even an employee of I don't know how many years – is a bit biased, so I asked them, his colleagues, his customers. They all said they knew him so well, had known him for years, but the man they knew was someone else – completely different. A made-up person.

'Horace Doncaster, well what can I say? He was always so kind, so generous,' they said. 'He'll be sorely missed.' Well, they might say that mightn't they, because they only wanted what he wanted to give, for a price mind you. Oh yes, he'd give them a book off the dusty old shelves in that damn shop of his when he'd found them some precious rare edition and charged them an absolute fortune. Oh yes, he'd give them a little extra, a gift, free, gratis and for nothing as a token of his great esteem. Of course he did; he was only too happy to offload some obscure volume nobody would ever want. Glad to get rid of them, he was. One less book to dust he used to say. One less book for me to dust, he should have said.

Oh yes, he'd offer them a complimentary freshly brewed coffee while they discussed the next possible purchase, it was all part of the service. That was my job, making the coffee, working the computer (he never figured that out) and dusting those ancient books. The Antiquarian Stock, he called them, but to me they were just dusty old books. The ones I had liked were those in the back of the shop out of the way, never seen by customers. They were children's books dating from the late 1800s to the 1930s. First editions, lots of them. Belonged to some relation of his, long dead no doubt, the name written on the flyleaves in that old-fashioned loopy writing, 'Theodore Doncaster.' After the bookseller went home to his large empty house, I'd stay on in the shop for a bit and open the boxes to look at those books. Books that children would have read and loved, but were now abandoned, unwanted. I started to research on the net to find out about the authors, and I discovered that the books were wanted. Very much so, judging by the prices they could fetch. Some of these books were worth serious money, but he wouldn't sell them. 'Waiting for the right market,' he said when I asked. There were people out there waiting with good money, but my suggestions fell on deaf ears. What did I know about business and markets? My job was dusting, and making fresh, ground coffee.

But while they sipped their aromatic Colombian brew, and murmured obsequious thanks as he slipped an extra book into their bags, those customers never saw him give a cup of coffee to the old man sitting on the bench on the other side of the road, outside the underground station. The old man who sat patiently waiting for his wife to come home. The wife who died in an accident on the underground ten years ago. No, they never saw him give that poor, sad old man a single cup of coffee to warm him up, because he never did – that's why. But they didn't ever see him not give the poor chap anything, if you see what I mean.

They probably didn't even notice the hunched figure on the old wooden seat, in his worn, grey overcoat. They would come off the train, into the shop, browse around, take books off the shelves and put them back in the wrong place. They would have lofty conversations with the erudite man wearing half-moon glasses and a silk cravat, who stood behind the polished wooden counter, but they didn't notice the man shivering outside on the old seat as they left the shop, pulling their collars up round their ears and unfurling their umbrellas, clutching their precious new purchase.

The bookseller, he was no mere shop-keeper, spent his days in his shop, surrounded by thousands of books and millions and millions of words, but never did he once spare a single word for that old man on the bench. Never did he ask him to come in to share the warmth of his shop, not even on the coldest or wettest of days. The thing is, both men were remarkably similar. About the same unidentifiable age, tall and thin and stooping. And both sad and lonely.

The customers may have been oblivious, but plenty of people did notice the bench man. All the locals, we talked to Ted. We stopped for a few words, brought him the odd treat of a hot drink, or a home-made cake, a new pair of gloves, or a scarf when the weather was bitter. He always thanked us politely, said we were kind and thoughtful, and made a complimentary comment about our new coat, our smile, our dog; whatever he could think of. Some of us had tried to persuade him to wait for her in the warm, but no, he couldn't do that, she would be expecting him to be there to escort her home. So every day from two in the afternoon until six o' clock he would wait patiently in all weathers. And when I turned the shop sign to say 'closed', pulled the window blinds down and turned the lights off, I would see the tall, bent figure push himself up from the bench, look toward the station one last time and then turn away as he slowly made his way back to his shabby little room above the launderette, another wrinkle of sadness etched on his face.

I remember the afternoon that things changed. I glanced up and saw an empty bench. It was twenty past two. The sad old man was no longer waiting. It was the woman who ran the launderette who told us, exploding into the dusty quietness of the shop.

'Ted's gone, poor man,' she gasped, breathless and shocked. 'I found him sitting in front of an old single-bar electric fire, not switched on. No gas nor electric,' she told us. 'Nothing. Place was colder than a tomb. Perhaps just a bit of warmth from the machines and that downstairs, but nothing more. Would you believe it? Got a brother somewhere apparently. Landlord's trying to get hold of him.' My employer made no comment but barked an order at me to stop gossiping.

When the old man from the bench died, crowds of people turned up to his funeral. Ted's passing wasn't unnoticed. People came to pay their respects, people whose names he may have once known but had long forgotten, people he didn't really know at all but who he'd talked to and who'd talked to him. But the old man who looked like him, the one who owned the bookshop, no, he didn't go to the funeral. As the vicar led the brief service for Theodore Doncaster, co-owner of Doncaster's Books we discovered that his own brother had stayed away from his funeral. Instead, he stayed in his shop, their shop, and arranged for a premium selection of first editions and sought-after volumes of children's books to be auctioned. I can't remember the exact figure they brought in now, but it was thousands. That was the right time? The right market?

And now it's his own funeral and the crematorium is almost empty. There are just a handful of us locals who were here a couple of months ago for the funeral of his twin, a paltry number of his bookish colleagues and two customers, who want to assess the stock in his shop. There were plenty of messages from other customers saying what a clever and wonderful man he was and how they'll miss him but, no, they can't make it to his funeral because they're so busy, things to do and places to go, but he'll be missed, very much. By the way, can you recommend another bookseller? It wasn't every day you met someone like him, was it. They don't make them like that anymore, do they?

And so I give my eulogy. I tell the people in the congregation about the virtues of Mr Horace Doncaster, bookseller. I tell them what little I know about his life, his Oxford education, his knowledge of books, his business acumen. I tell them that he was a respected authority on his subject, that he had written many papers and knew a great deal, but that it was those of us who lived in his community, who really knew what he was like. We saw the manner in which he treated his twin brother, a sad and lonely old man, mad with grief, which demonstrated to us what sort of person he really was. The booksellers and customers nod their heads approvingly, of course Horace would have done the right thing for an unfortunate, crazy brother. Let's get this over with.

I look at the other people, those who understand my words. They know that they do make them like they always did. Made up people.

The Old Wife's Tale

Jeremy Bath was desperate and confused. There was only a week and a day left before the presentation. Facts and figures, figures and facts; his head was all a jigger.

Queen Bee, Dr Maggie Schmitt, Head of Psychology at York University, glared: 'What's the matter Jeremy, why do you keep looking at your watch?'

'I'm going to be late for work,' he said, and blushed, trying not to stare at the red lace bra peeping over the top of her low-cut dress.

'So what do you do when you're not studying?' she asked.

'I'm a motorbike courier.'

She raised her black pencilled eyebrows. Jeremy was used to that sort of reaction. Perhaps it was his thick glasses; not suited to a crazy biker screaming into the night, the wind slapping against his face. A powerful man who gathered protesting women into his arms, he dreamt of women often – even Maggie Schmitt — slung over a desk, skirt raised...

'You've missed the point, Jeremy.' Maggie Schmitt looked up from the thick pile of research papers. 'You've got some interesting ideas but you haven't convinced me that you've got to the heart of what it is that women really want.' She smiled; a crack of a smile that stayed in her mouth.

'Can't you be more specific; can't you just tell me what's missing?'

She tapped a pen on the desk. 'I'm not here to do the work for you. You've had nearly a year; it should be finished by now.' She handed him the papers. 'This is your last chance. Mess this up and you're out, off the course.'

Failure for Jeremy was a sentence worse than death. Death when it finally came was swift; failure was like a barnacle attaching itself to a shell, cemented and perpetual. Tiny specks of rain like needles tapped against the window. The psychology department, with its distinctive chequerboard rotunda, overlooked a large lake surrounded by weeping willows. He watched as a man, dressed in a raincoat, threw a stick into the water. A small furry dog chased after it, and clutching it in its mouth paddled like crazy to stay afloat.

'The only thing I can suggest,' said Maggie, putting a red line through Jeremy's name, 'is that you interview a few more women; preferably older than twenty-five!' There was a knock at the door. 'Come in!'

Jeremy gathered his papers; some fell to the floor, Maggie sighed. He headed towards the door.

'Good luck,' she said.

The rain lashed down, making vision difficult. Jeremy's motorbike drowned out the hum of slow-moving traffic. At this time of day, it was better to go via Nunnery Lane to Theatre Royal, rather than up Tower Street where the roads would be packed with wandering tourists. If he had time to spare, he liked to walk round the city, even treat himself to one of the sights. He raced towards the lights, screeching to a halt as they turned red. His favourite was the Castle Museum, especially on a hot day. When exploring the old prisons he often found himself drawn to the condemned cell. Standing against a cold brick wall, he would imagine himself as the notorious, flamboyant Dick Turpin, waiting fearlessly in the dark before being hanged. With a flick of the throttle, he sped past the station towards Lendal Bridge; in the distance he could see the theatre.

Jeremy came in from the rain, through a stage door at the side of the theatre. Removing his helmet, he nodded at the doorman. 'Package for J.J. Jensen.' He brushed the water from his leathers.

'Up there,' the doorman indicated to a short flight of stairs. 'See the stage manager, he'll know where Ms Jensen is.'

He climbed the stairs and waited backstage. The smells of wood and sweat reminded Jeremy of the Bletchley Park Amateur Dramatic Society and Jenni Atkinson. Just her name still made him shiver. It had all been so wonderful when it began. Teenage sweethearts: Jenni and Jeremy - perfect. Two leading lights on the stage. Jenni was a born actress and beautiful too. Two magical summers. They were madly in love. He'd even imagined they might get married one day; until her eighteenth birthday. He had wanted to make it so special. Took her to a French restaurant. She had veal and he had Steak Tartare and of course a bottle of champagne.

They stopped by some fields on the way home. It was a warm and balmy evening. Jenni took off her cardigan, folding it into a makeshift pillow, and laid down amidst the buttercups. She unbuttoned the top three buttons on her dress. It was obvious; at last she was ready. It was amazing making love with Jenni that night; at least it had been, until one forty-five the next afternoon when he rang and her mother answered.

'You've got a nerve ringing here. Jenni doesn't want to speak to you.' The line went dead.

Almost instantly his world shattered. She wouldn't even reply to his letters. Some weeks later he overheard some girls whispering at a bus stop. He heard Jenni's name and the word 'rape,' and put two and two together. And after that Jeremy stayed away from women. Women, he had decided, could eat you up and spit you out like a pip, like a sour bitter pip.

Jeremy found himself watching a rather wondrous sight and couldn't believe his luck; it quite took his breath away. A group of semi-naked nymphs were dancing round an old woman.

A man banged a clipboard. 'Great.' He looked at his watch. 'Tea time.'

One by one, the nymphs floated off the stage. The old hag stood up, rubbing her back and stretching her arms in the air. Jeremy ran over to the man with the clipboard. 'Parcel for Miss Jensen.'

'There,' he pointed at the old woman.

She smiled and walked towards them. Jeremy handed her the parcel.

She studied him; 'Do I know you?'

'I don't think so,' Jeremy felt uncomfortable under her gaze.

'Shouldn't I sign something?'

He nodded, pulling a piece of paper from inside his leather jacket.

'Follow me,' she said, marching across the stage.

'I've got a pen here!' he shouted after her, but she ignored him.

He followed her round the back of the stage, past a girl in overalls painting scenery and a group of young lads lifting a large canvas. Jeremy had an idea. Maybe this Miss Jensen could help. She looked at least sixty, an actress, must have been around a bit in her youth. He would ask her.

She disappeared through a doorway. The room was full of brightly coloured outfits. Photos of actors and actresses, some in colour, some in black and white adorned the walls. She picked up a pen from a dressing table, and signed the form.

'Here we are.' She handed it back.

He coughed. Women in the flesh always made him nervous even old ones. He coughed again. 'I was wondering, perhaps you, ermm...'

'Do you want my autograph?' Her stony eyes widened. Her face was ravaged, wrinkled, and caked in orange make-up and her crooked nose had a large bump on the ridge. The hair was grey, it looked like a wig; god she was ugly.

'The thing is...'

'Oh for goodness sake spit it out.'

'I'm doing a presentation next week at the university. The theme is 'Relationships and Sexuality in the Twenty-First Century.' I know what men want,' he smiled. She didn't smile back. 'But when it comes to women,' he shrugged, 'I've questioned over a hundred of them in the last year but they all seem to want something different. Some want financial security, some want fun in bed, some want separate houses, and some just want to be pampered and flattered. I'm totally confused and if I don't work it out, I'm a dead man. Do you know what women *really* want in a relationship?'

She laughed. 'Of course I do, but don't you have a pretty young wife to help you?'

Jeremy shook his head.

'Girlfriend?'

He was silent.

'Supposing I help you,' she said. 'What do I get in return?'

'I'd do anything, I'm desperate. Trim the hedge, sweep the path, fix things, anything.'

'Anything?' Walking towards the door, she added, 'You promise?'

Jeremy followed nodding.

Closing the door she smiled. 'So you'd marry me then?'

He laughed. 'Of course.' He was beginning to relax.

Jeremy was coming to the end of his presentation. It had gone so well until now. The more he tried, the more the words got stuck in his mouth and only bits of them wiggled out. He'd lost his place. Hundreds of staring eyes waited. Maggie Schmitt, sitting next to the Dean, smiled – one of her impatient smiles. He recovered himself; the spidery scribble became clear.

'What makes women happy?' He sounded authoritative. 'What do women really want in a relationship?' He looked over at Maggie. 'A woman wants to be king and queen over her lover, her partner, her mate. Woe betide the man or woman who tries to dominate her. Sovereignty and control; that, ladies and gentlemen, is what women want.' He paused. 'Thank you.'

For a moment there was silence. And suddenly clapping and roars of approval filled the hall. Most of the women were standing and cheering. Maggie Schmitt walked onto the stage.

She whispered, 'Looks like you're off the hook.' Speaking into the microphone, she began, 'Quiet now.' The noise subsided. 'Well done Jeremy.' Turning back to the audience she asked, 'Any questions?'

A woman shouted: 'If a man makes a promise, do you think he should honour it?'

'I most certainly do.'

Jeremy looked towards the back of the hall in the direction of the voice. It was the old hag from the theatre. What was she doing here? A few heads turned.

'You promised to do anything if I helped you. I asked you to marry me and you said yes.' There was a splatter of giggles from the audience. 'Remember?'

'Well?' said Maggie Schmitt. 'Did you promise to marry this woman?'

Jeremy looked at his tutor and back at the old woman. 'Well, it was a joke. I didn't mean it.'

'My car's outside,' shouted the old woman. 'It'll only take us a couple of hours to get to Gretna Green.'

The audience began to chant: 'Je-re-my, Je-re-my.'

'A promise is a promise,' said Maggie. 'You'll have to go.'

Surely, the old bag wouldn't go through with it. Jeremy laughed and waved at the audience. He was getting into the spirit of it. By the door, he held out his arm. The old woman curtseyed and took it. They left the hall together.

They sat at a table in The Orange Duck Hotel. In one of the

corners of the room, there was a patch of damp on the pink flowered wallpaper. The smell of cheap air-freshener made Jeremy's nose tingle.

'So, here we are,' said the old woman, finishing the last of her haddock.

Jeremy was on edge. Why had he agreed to a date?

Suddenly, the room was plunged into darkness. Her face brushed against his. He felt sick; she was all rubbery and wrinkly. She pulled at his trousers.

'Enough,' he cried, leaping up from the table.

'What is it, what's the matter?'

'I can't,' he said. 'I can't do it.' He couldn't see her face properly in the dark but it was etched into his memory. 'You're too old.' He sneezed three times.

'Now you listen to me young man, I saved your bacon. Anyway, I've got a good figure for my age.' She pulled up her skirt. 'Look at my legs.' Jeremy closed his eyes. 'Just imagine this,' she moved towards him, resting her cheek against his chest, 'I could stay like this, old. You would always be confident of my faithfulness and love for you.'

He moved away.

'Or I could become a beautiful young woman with many admirers.' She flung her arms in the air and pirouetted. 'You might become jealous, not sure of my faithfulness.' She cackled like a witch. 'Think carefully. Which would you prefer?'

Jeremy sat back down, he was tired. 'You decide,' he said just as the lights came on.

'Right answer,' said the old woman and ran into a nearby toilet.

When she came out, even without his glasses, Jeremy was startled. He grabbed his glasses from his breast pocket; before him was not an old woman, but a nymph-like creature with long dark hair. Older, yes, but he recognised her, 'Jenni Atkinson,' he said.

'The future wife of Jeremy Bath now.'

And now he recognised her voice. In her hand was a grey wig.

'Make-up! You're so short-sighted you didn't even notice. J.J. Jensen is my stage name. I often wondered what happened to you.' For a moment there was silence. 'I'm so sorry, about all that misunderstanding, it was my mother.

She found the contraceptives in my bag and went bonkers. She wouldn't let me out of the house for weeks - I nearly died of shame.'

She wrapped herself around him. 'Forgive me?'

The Reading Group

'Morning all.' The fat man heaves himself on to the bus.

'Morning,' chorus the three old ladies, giggling excitedly.

The bus trundles down the steep road, passing rows of oh, such neat little bungalows, swept and brushed into immaculate order like lines of pedigree dogs waiting for their moment at Crufts. Every now and again a figure emerges in the road waving a stick, at which signal the bus stops obediently and minutes pass as the newcomer settles down. Groundhog Day has begun.

I am particularly depressed this morning. My wife started it. Lately we've been having a lot of spats.

'If you're doing nothing at lunchtime,' she began.

'Actually, I'm busy, the shop depends on me.'

'I know dear, but it's only a charity shop. I've got a late meeting and I wondered if you could get some supper in.'

Only a charity shop! That's how she sees my worth. Just because she works all hours God sends she thinks I am good for nothing. Made redundant at fifty eight, what can I do? The charity shop occupies me three days a week, and my main source of pride and satisfaction, my reading group, meets monthly. I am useless. My wife smiles brightly at me, crinkling up her lined face, and the grey in her once luxuriant hair fills me with a sudden surge of pity and shame.

All is about to change, however. Jenny bares her gap-toothed grimace at me and I nod back. How I long for nubile youth. It's my turn to sort and bag out the clothing and other donated items, a task I quite enjoy. I am deciding how to price three Shrek CDs when a voice trills in my ear.

'Hi, you must be David, I'm Liza. Jenny told me to ask for you, she said you'd know what was what.'

She can't be a day over eighteen, and while not conventionally pretty there's something about her green eyes and freckles that reminds me of my wife, in the salad days of our marriage. My stomach clenches for a moment and I am conscious of my developing paunch and my jowly face which must be red from bending over the CDs. She smiles, I am thrown back into the past, and I am lost.

She looks round the shop critically, and I see it through her eyes, the books haphazardly thrust on to shelves, boxes lying in wait to trip up the unwary, musty clothes in a heap in the backroom. It is her first day but she marches up to Jenny and proposes a complete reorganisation.

Surprisingly she is given a cautious go-ahead. 'Get David to help you. He will know what is appropriate.'

I am only too willing. I find Liza quick and co-operative. The reorganisation takes several days and we work companionably together. Time passes quickly now and I begin to wonder what Liza thinks of me, if she, like my wife, sees me as a no-hoper.

One day I find her in tears behind the Barbara Cartlands. I put my arm around her in an avuncular way.

'What is it, my dear?'

She turns her head into my shoulder and I pat it comfortingly, running my fingers through the tangled black curls.

'It's Nick, my boyfriend. He says he doesn't want to see me so much, that he needs space. I think he's trying to dump me.'

I am bracing. 'That doesn't mean a thing. I know men. I am one after all,' (self-deprecating laugh), 'give him space, don't be available whenever he is, play him at his own game, best of all...' here I'm on a roll, 'go out with someone else, see if he likes that!'

Astonishingly she obeys me. A week after this exchange we are in the back together, she sorting through woolly jumpers, me checking men's trousers, when she ups and hugs me.

'You were so right, Dave, I went clubbing with some friends, didn't tell Nick, and met this really cool guy, Jason, and I've told Nick he can eff off whenever he wants to.'

Now my days at the shop are entirely different. Liza and I have established a special relationship. She looks up to me and I look after her. Then one afternoon: 'Dave, you read a lot, don't you? Have you ever tried to write anything?' A coy glance. 'You know so much, have lived so long.'

As it happens I once tried to write a novel but lacked the application.

'Good try Liza,' I say, 'but no, I don't want to write.' I hesitate. 'I do run a reading group though.' Impulsively,

'Maybe you would be interested and come along one evening?'

The moment I say it I am terrified. What have I done? She will laugh; the sad old git she will think.

She smiles at me. 'Perhaps I will.'

I want to take her in my arms and kiss her gratefully. She looks so pretty, a flesh and blood Venus among the plastic bric-a-brac.

'That's wonderful, you've made my day.'

Puzzled but pleased she is so sweet. 'It's nothing.'

Nothing? She doesn't understand.

'It means a lot to me,' I say.

Running a group needs a firm hand at the tiller, although there are only five of us. At the last meeting, there was a mini-rebellion. Only I and jolly Janet wanted to read Jane Austen, and I was forced to use my prerogative as chairman to insist on reading *Emma* the following month. Michael actually called me a pretentious twit for forcing the issue, provoking a snigger from the others, and although everyone eventually agreed with the decision, there was a bit of bad feeling towards the end which rather upset me. Now I tell Liza about it (omitting the pretentious bit) and she is very sympathetic.

'You tell them,' she says. 'I loved *Pride and Prejudice* when I was young.' Then, shyly, pleading with her lovely eyes, 'I wonder if Jason...could he come as well? I'm sure he could learn so much from you.'

I am dismayed. I do not want to share Liza with Jason. I take my time, sorting through a bound set of Shakespeare's plays and wondering how much they might fetch. I am weighing out the Henrys and putting them in chronological order, when I drop one on Liza's foot. She is wearing open-toed sandals and screams in agony. By the time I have apologized and comforted her, I have agreed that she and Jason will attend the October meeting.

It is 7.00 pm, Friday 12th October. Michael arrives with the others, regretting his comments last time. I am gracious and wish Liza were here to witness my magnanimity. I am fretting about her when there is a ring at the doorbell. A languid youth in his late twenties, with holes where his jeans should be, is smirking at me. He is handsome in a rough, unkempt sort of way, with shaggy hair that gleams gold in the lamplight.

'Hi,' he says, 'you must be Dave, mate.'

'I am David Keane, yes.'

'Great, I'm Jason.' He waves a paw at me and steps forward. 'Sorry we're late.'

My heart thuds painfully as I see Liza peeping out behind him. She is wearing a shiny bomber jacket thing and her long legs are encased in tight-fitting jeans.

'Come in.' I am mumbling like a teenager.

He pushes past me into the hall, raises an eyebrow as if to ask the way, and moves towards the sound of voices. I follow with a sinking heart as he heads straight for my chair which I had placed strategically at the front of my carefully arranged semicircle and plonks himself down on it. I offer to take Liza's jacket, but she refuses and sits on the floor at his feet. I pull up another, rather uncomfortable chair, and introduce them both.

'Don't worry if this is a bit overwhelming,' I say in a kindly way. 'You can just listen if you want. As you know, we shall be discussing *Emma*.'

Jason looks round the group. 'Yeah, the snob.'

'Oh, how I agree with you.' Shy little Graham is leaning forward in his chair and Ted is nodding vigorously. Michael says nothing but his eyes are swivelling as he watches the group's reactions to this presumptuous intervention.

'What's wrong with that?' Janet asks in a puzzled way. 'She's clearly a better class than some of the others.'

'Up the workers!' shouts Ted irrelevantly.

I try to speak. I have prepared carefully for this meeting, with A-level notes gleaned from the internet. 'Order, order,' I say loudly but Jason takes no notice. He launches into a speech about the socio-economic context of the book and soon is virtually running a seminar. I try to intervene but they are all hanging onto Jason's words like flies round a pile of dung.

I can see Liza gazing at Jason adoringly and need to do something, to reassert my natural authority. At 8.15pm I say, 'Sorry to break it up so early, but I have a busy day ahead. Now next time I'd like us to do something completely different.' I lay my copy of *Moby Dick* on the coffee table. 'I shall be happy to prepare an introduction.'

'Why can't we do Jeffery Archer?' asks Ted. 'He's a clever

bloke.'

'Really,' I begin, but oh yes, bloody Jason comes in again. 'Have you read *Moby Dick*?'

'Not yet, that's the point of a reading group,' I respond sarcastically.

'Well, I have, and unless you're heavily into whaling I don't recommend it.'

'I agree,' says Michael unexpectedly. 'I think we need more time for this decision process. The last choice,' he looks at me, his eyes glinting coldly behind his spectacles, 'was hardly democratic. I'm sorry you're so busy Dave but why don't the rest of you come back to my house, and we can have a few beers and finish the discussion properly. Of course, Dave, if you find you're not too busy after all, you can join us.'

I am mortified. Of course I can't join them.

'Perhaps you'd like to host the next meeting, Michael?' I'm confident he won't want the responsibility.

'Gladly.' He shows his teeth.

Someone is laughing mockingly. It is Jason, his arm wrapped possessively round Liza's shoulders. I look at her and she is laughing with him, turning her head away when I try to catch her eye.

'That sounds good,' she says.

As if in a film, I watch myself turn slowly towards Jason and hit him in the face.

I am lying on the floor with a bloody nose and tears are flowing down my cheeks. They have all gone, and my wife is kneeling beside me, holding a cloth to my face.

'What on earth were you thinking of?' she scolds. 'Fighting at your age. And over Jane Austen too. You might have been hurt.'

'I am hurt.' The words come out muffled. I raise my head with her help and look into her kindly, tired eyes.

'I do love you, you know, you silly man,' she says, and in the warmth of her smile I see Liza in her, or perhaps her in Liza, and know the truth of it and what she really means to me.

'Did I do him any damage,' I ask hopefully.

'Which one?' she asks. 'Nothing they won't recover from.'

I begin to feel anxious. She reads my mind. 'Janet, Graham and Ted have asked me to let you know they will be here for the November meeting. I gather you're going to read *Moby Dick*. They said they'd give Michael's invitation a miss.'

She strokes my hand. 'Don't let the reading group upset you. You're worth twenty of them.'

I am about to ask about Liza's reaction, but change my mind. It doesn't seem important now. 'Only twenty?' I ask.

Crazy in Love

It was already dark outside. Eve Bailey, a willowy brunette in her late twenties, opened the match box and carefully lit the candles in the silver candleholder. Satisfied, she secured a strand of chestnut brown hair behind her ear. The warm flicker of the candles was all the dinner table needed. Now it looked just perfect – festive and welcoming.

'Stella,' she called and quickly placed pepper and salt next to the dishes. 'Dinner is ready.'

Once seated, her sister closed her eyes and slowly inhaled the aromatic flavours wafting up from the roasted meat and vegetables.

'This smells absolutely delicious,' she said and started to fill her plate. 'And these rosemary potatoes look fantastic. I wish I could cook like you.' Questioningly she looked at Eve who sat silently in front of her plate and sipped some red wine. 'Don't you want to eat anything?'

'No,' her sister replied. 'Somehow I've lost my appetite.'

'No wonder, so shortly after Father's death,' Stella said. 'Besides, this was his favourite dish. It's so sad that he can't be with us tonight.'

Strained, Eve lifted her wine glass to her mouth. Two days had passed by since the funeral, two long days. Her head bent, she had stood in the cemetery chapel and had looked down at her black patent leather shoes.

Impatiently she tapped the tip of her left shoe onto the floor. The service just didn't seem to end. They should long be on their way to the grave. From outside, through the wooden doors, she could hear the faint sound of people talking. The mourners for the next funeral must be already congregating in front of the chapel.

Scrunching up her white lace handkerchief, she threw a careful glance at her sister who stood next to her, sobbing and her eyes red from all the crying. Eve sighed. Stella loved our father, she thought, unlike me. That's why I don't manage to cry. With knitted brows she stared at the dry handkerchief in her left hand. And why should I have loved him when he always furtively observed me as if I was one of his patients in the asylum? She shivered. His strange questions and the worried look when he heard my reply – all a test to find out whether I was not quite sane. Did he really think I hadn't noticed?

Expressionless she had looked at the flower-bedecked oak coffin that stood next to the altar and seemed almost majestic with its gleaming brass fittings. My own father believed me to be crazy, she thought, to be a cold-blooded psychopath. As if I could hurt a fly. A fine smile twitched around the corners of her mouth. At least now no-one forced her to swallow the little white pills her father had prescribed for her.

After the funeral party had solemnly marched to the open grave, led by the coffin bearers and the vicar in his wafting robe, the latter spread his arms and started to pray. Eve stood with folded hands next to her sister on the gravel path and, her eyes hidden under the wide brim of her hat, scanned the faces of the relatives and friends who had turned up to pay their last respects to their father. Wearing mourning, they looked dull and unremarkable as if they didn't want to upstage the coffin under the colourful splendour of the flower arrangement. Several faces seemed vaguely familiar, others she didn't know at all. Since childhood Eve and Stella had avoided family reunions of any kind, and nobody had forced them to attend.

That's what you get, she thought. I'm nearly thirty and don't know my next of kin.

Just as she turned her attention back to the grave, she spotted HIM in the midst of the mourners, tall with dark hair and distinctive good looks. Across the heads of the others he looked straight into her eyes, and his glance hit her like an electric shock. Eve felt the tell-tale touch of butterfly wings below her heart. Her lower lip started to tremble. Love at first sight – so it did exist after all. She had never believed that cupid's arrow could really strike within seconds. Now she knew better.

This must be fate, she thought. Father leaves my life, and HE enters – the man of my dreams. The one I've always waited for.

The realisation almost took her breath away: her true love stood so close on the gravel path, and she had no clue who he was.

'Earth to earth, ashes to ashes, dust to dust,' muttered the vicar and handed her sister a small shovel. Quietly crying, Stella stepped forward to the grave and threw a rose onto the coffin. Then she shovelled a bit of earth on top and returned to her place on the path. Eve followed her example. Her thoughts danced like drunken goblins through her head, back and forth, up and down. Who was this man? The tense cemetery ambiance and an unprecedented feeling of joy, the sultry sweetness of wilting flowers and blazing lust all combined in the overwhelming desire to have him. Just for herself.

She took a rose from the vase next to the grave, the age-old symbol of love and passion. For a short moment she smelled the bewitching scent the flower exuded and then threw it down onto the coffin. The situation didn't allow her to hand the rose to the dark-haired man. Her head bent, she stepped back next to her sister. Visibly shaken and with tears in her eyes, Stella waited for the condolences of the other mourners. Eve's eyes glistened. She waited for HIM.

The one who knocks you off your feet. She had never been able to grasp what this might possibly mean. Until today. The exact moment when his hand touched hers, Eve's world came apart at the seams. The ground beneath her started to sway, the birds interrupted their song and even the cemetery and the darkly robed mourning party around her didn't seem to exist any more. All that remained were him and her, nothing else. Without saying anything she looked at him dreamily, her hand still in his. Blue, she thought. His eyes are as blue as a summer sky above the sea.

She was shocked when he retreated and turned to Stella. Terrified she held her breath. He mustn't leave before I've found out his name. Oh God, don't let him go.

'Please come to the reception at our house after the funeral,' she uttered but couldn't be sure whether he had heard. The next mourner already stood in front of her to offer his condolences.

He hadn't heard, at least he wasn't at the reception. A champagne flute in her hand, Eve thrust her way through the crowd in search of him but it was no good. He hadn't come. Little pearls of sweat formed on her forehead. This can't be happening, she thought. I can't possibly have lost him forever. With shaking fingers, she raised the glass to her mouth. Someone here must know him.

She was not in luck. Nobody knew him or had seen him. Nobody even seemed to remember that a tall, dark-haired man had attended the funeral. In the memory of the others he simply didn't exist. Heavily she sank into an armchair and abandoned herself to the effect of the alcohol and the abysmal hopelessness that had taken possession of her.

'Look,' she heard her sister whisper to a distant cousin. 'Eve is crying. Thank God she's finally allowing herself to show her feelings, I was worried about her. It's not good to bottle up your feelings.'

The cousin nodded. 'Time heals all wounds,' she said and threw her a compassionate glance. 'Poor thing, she must have been very fond of him.'

But Eve didn't mourn her father, didn't even care that they had just buried him. She cried about the only thing in the world that she had ever truly desired, the tall, dark-haired man with the stunning blue eyes.

After dinner Stella took her daily bath – a ritual that could last hours. Meanwhile Eve stood by the living room window, holding her glass of red wine and looking outside. She felt a shiver of excitement run down her spine. If everything went to plan, she'd meet the man of her dreams again very shortly – but what could possibly go wrong now? Her glance fell upon the golden angel who seemed to float in the air above the local church tower, blowing his trumpet. From afar he almost looked like cupid with his love arrow. Eve raised her glass of wine and gave him a cheer. Of course everything will go to plan, she thought. And this time I won't let the man of my dreams get away.

Mozart's wonderful *Serenata Notturna* wafted from the bathroom over to her. Beautiful. This music was to simply die for. Slowly she turned, went through the open double doors, then across the hallway and nearer and nearer to the bathroom. The hint of a smile played around the corners of her mouth when she put her hand on the handle.

Indeed, she thought, and opened the door. Simply to die for.

'May I offer my heartfelt condolences, Miss Bailey,' said the undertaker who was dressed in dignified black. It was the same man who had already advised her after the death of her father.

'I read about the tragic accident in the papers. One hears so often about casualties in the bathroom.'

Eve glanced down at her folded hands. 'I don't wish to talk about this,' she whispered while the gentleman in black discreetly pushed a brochure with a selection of coffins across the table.

'Would you prefer oak or rather something else?'

Forty minutes later she stepped back onto the pavement. Relieved, she took a deep breath of fresh air. It had been oppressively stuffy inside. The pleasant light breeze outside was a relief.

It couldn't possibly have gone better, she thought. The funeral would be on Wednesday, exactly like Father's. She looked up into the sunny autumn sky. Somewhere up there an angel called Stella flew through the clouds, just like the one above the church tower.

'Sorry Stella,' she said quietly in the direction of the sky. 'But how else could I have possibly made the love of my life come back to me?' She swiped a strand of hair off her face that the wind had blown there. 'If he's come to Father's funeral, then he will certainly also come to yours. You do understand that, don't you?'

A single sycamore leaf blew across the street and got caught by the tip of her shoe. A sign. Stella had answered. Eve smiled. She had known all along that her sister would understand.

Who wouldn't?

Roses for Jane

It was very early in the morning for someone to be ringing my front doorbell. I jumped out of bed and flung on my dressing-gown.

'Jane Davies?' the delivery man asked. He was holding a box of long-stemmed red roses.

'Why yes,' I answered, bleary eyed and in shock. 'Are those for me?'

'They certainly are; that is if you are Ms Jane Davies. Somebody loves you,' he grinned.

I signed his clip board and he winked and handed me the flowers. I closed the door and opened the little card. It read: 'To my darling Jane, love from Denis.'

The only Denis I knew was the computer manager at work, Denis Peeks; why would he be sending me flowers? Then I noticed that the card was heart-shaped. One glance at the calendar confirmed it was Valentine's Day. What a wonderful surprise, I thought. I had known Denis for about a year and had always fancied him, but he had never even hinted that he liked me. Even so, I was delighted with this gesture. I hadn't had a date for ages, and it would be nice to go out with someone so lovely.

There had been some offers, but they were from men I didn't fancy or who were probably married. I wasn't interested in going down that road. Denis seemed different. Tall, blond and reasonably good looking, he had a very pleasant way about him and was quiet and unassuming. He was about thirty-five, and I knew he was single and lived on a new development on the outskirts of town.

Suddenly my alarm clock went off, startling me; time to get dressed. I put the roses in water and started to prepare for work. My dark red hair fell loosely about my shoulders. Usually I'd put it up in a knot, but today I would leave it loose. I was running late by the time I reached the office.

'Have you been ploughing through your Valentine cards?' Julie, my secretary, asked as I walked into the office.

'No...well, yes. I could hardly get out of the front door!' I answered, smiling inwardly. I'd keep the roses a secret between Denis and myself. I lowered my head to my computer and waited. Maybe Denis would pass through the office today.

'Then I can thank him for the flowers,' I thought. Perhaps I could follow him out so that no-one would hear us. Would he ask me out? My imagination was working overtime. It was very hard to concentrate, and I couldn't wait any longer; I asked Julie if Denis was in today.

'Denis is in the computer room,' she said.

I got a file from my desk and went to the door marked 'IT support'. When I entered, Denis was sitting at one of the computers. The background on his screen was a picture of beautiful flowers.

'That's lovely,' I said.

'It's from Monet's garden,' he said looking up, as if surprised to see me. But a lovely smile crinkled up his blue eyes. 'I like flowers, they brighten up my day.'

'Me too,' I agreed, smiling back at him.

'I could copy this onto your screen if you like,' he offered.

'I'd love that – and thank you for the flowers,' I said. I waited for him to say something, but he didn't. Perhaps it was because there were others in the room. On impulse, I decided to invite him to dinner. There was no time like the present. After all, it was Valentine's Day and he had made the first move. Leaning over, I whispered the invitation. 'By way of a thank you,' I added.

He looked up at me with a puzzled expression but readily accepted.

'Why yes,' he said, 'but what about your family?'

'I have my own house, small but cosy,' I replied, 'and I like cooking.'

And just like that it was arranged.

Denis arrived carrying a bottle of wine and a bunch of mixed flowers.

'More flowers!' I couldn't believe it. He was a real romantic. 'You shouldn't have done that; sending the roses was enough.'

'Roses?' he repeated, looking confused. 'Not guilty.'

I laughed uneasily; he was teasing, or was he?

He looked towards the vase. 'I'm afraid I can't take the credit for those – unfortunately.'

'But then, who? Look at the card.'

'I see – but it wasn't me, honestly. I only wish it was.' He looked embarrassed. 'This is why you invited me, isn't it? I feel as though I'm here under false pretences.'

'But I thanked you for the flowers at work!' I spluttered, my face turning crimson.

'I thought you meant the flowers on the computer,' he said. 'Do you want me to leave?'

'Of course not,' I felt embarrassed. 'I'm just a bit confused that's all and besides, I've already cooked us dinner.'

'It smells wonderful,' he said. 'Shall I open the wine?'

I nodded and Denis followed me into the kitchen. I indicated the glasses and he poured out the wine. Sipping the wine helped to calm me and we spent a very pleasant evening chatting and getting to know each other. He told me that he loved walking in the country, photography and nature. All things I enjoyed myself.

'Would you like to see some of my work?' he asked shyly.

'Yes, I'd love to,' I answered, suppressing the urge to add, when? 'What did you think when I invited you to dinner?' I asked. 'You must have thought I was very forward?'

'I was surprised, but I couldn't believe my luck. I had always thought you very reserved. At work you look so severe and business-like. No that sounds wrong...' Denis faltered, his blue eyes wide and sincere. 'Whoever this Denis is, he is the loser.' And then he smiled and his entire face changed, and my heart flipped.

The next morning I awoke with several questions on my mind. Who on earth could this other Denis be? Who had sent the roses? And was it a joke? If so it was an expensive joke. I just didn't understand. No matter who had sent the roses, they had done me a favour and helped break the ice with my Denis, I really liked him.

When I arrived at work Linda, a work experience girl, was standing in the reception by my office. It was obvious she was very upset.

'Whatever's wrong?' I asked.

'It's about the flowers,' she sobbed.

'You sent them?' I asked.

'Yes, from Mr Richardson.'

'Mr Richardson sent me roses?' Mr Richardson was about sixty and had been happily married for nearly forty years.

'Yes – No, they were from Mr Richardson. They should

have gone to his wife Jane, but I made a mistake. I'm so sorry.'

'I see,' I said.

'He said, "send roses to Jane for Valentine's Day," so I did,' she said teary-faced, a screwed-up tissue in her hand. 'I didn't know his wife was called Jane. I'm so sorry. He was furious when he found out.'

The error had been discovered that morning when Mr Richardson phoned the florist to find out what had happened to his wife's flowers. Later that day, Mr Richardson called me to apologise for any embarrassment.

'Please don't worry,' I told him. 'And don't be too hard on Linda; it was an easy mistake to make.'

'Oh, I can see the funny side of it now,' he replied. 'Although I have some making up to do with my Jane,' he laughed.

I wondered if my Denis had heard what had happened and later that same morning I rang his number, but got no reply.

'Anyone seen Denis Peeks?' I asked Julie.

'He isn't in today,' came the reply.

I gasped, hoping it wasn't my cooking that was the culprit – or was he avoiding me?

After work I tried Denis's home number but there was still no reply. I was worried. Why hadn't he phoned me? Perhaps he was ill at home. Was he blaming my cooking? Last night I had high hopes of a relationship; now I was just worried that I had poisoned him.

The next morning, the background of Monet's garden was on my computer and within a few minutes my door opened and in walked Denis.

'Are you okay?' I asked anxiously.

'Yes I'm fine; the planning meeting was gruelling but I survived.'

'Planning meeting?'

'Yes, the annual planning meeting where we're shut up for the day in the Grange Hotel without air, living on bread and water, and no phones,' he laughed.

'I forgot,' I said.

'I left you a message.' Denis looked amused.

I'd not checked my answer service; I must have been in a state.

'I thought I'd poisoned you,' I said nervously.

'No, no ill-effects. I don't know if you would be interested – look at this.' He stood, going from one foot to the other. 'I hope I'm not being too forward.'

Then he handed me a typed sheet of paper. I glanced down and saw that it contained the details of a weekend trip to Paris, including a visit to Monet's garden.

'My photographic club is organising it and you seemed so interested in the gardens. My sister is going, and you could share with her...' He paused.

'Sounds great. When is it? Did you hear about Linda and the flowers?' I rambled.

'It's not until June; you could come and meet the people and, well, I know you will get on with my sister; she's very friendly... What about Linda?' he asked.

We chatted on and I told him the full story of Linda's mistake with the flowers.

'A dozen red roses, eh?' He pretended to look concerned and then he laughed. 'I'll have to send her some.' He looked up at my shocked face. 'Well, she did me a big favour – maybe next Valentine's Day?' He grinned.

I gazed up into his lovely blue eyes and smiled.

'I can hardly wait,' I murmured.

'You may not have to,' he said and from behind his back, he produced a single red rose.

From Bagamoyo to Zanzibar by Dhow

Was that "Sudden and Unexpected Deaths" printed on the tattered red spine of that old, black foolscap notebook? Even more alarming, our names were being laboriously copied into it. Eventually, after a good deal of searching through rickety wooden drawers, a dusty stamp was produced which, with loud thumps, managed to print a faint round circle on each of our passports. We were now allowed exit from Tanganyika and entry into Zanzibar. Had nobody in Bagamoyo's Passport Office realised that Tanganyika and Zanzibar had united to form Tanzania five years before?

My heart skipped a beat as I recalled that, during the 18th and 19th centuries, slaves were imprisoned here before being transported at night by ship to the slave markets in Zanzibar. We had just learned this at the town's museum soon after we had been persuaded to take the dhow trip across the Indian Ocean to Zanzibar, but before we had noticed the rusty vestiges of chains embedded in concrete along the beach.

We had also found out that in 1874, after a nine month journey of 1,000 miles, David Livingstone's body had rested here in the Holy Cross church of Bagamoyo until the high tide came in to take him to Zanzibar en route to Westminster Abbey for burial.

Travelling by night, by dhow, to exotic Zanzibar had seemed like an exciting way to end our school holiday but now I wasn't so sure.

Our group consisted of six young teachers; three boys and three girls, for we were little more than that, doing our bit for education in 1969 Kenya and we had been joined that day by a slightly older, fresh-faced American, who was not what he seemed.

As arranged, we met Abdul our dhow-master under a starry sky on the beach. His flowing white robes glowed in the eerie light of a full moon and he was clutching a watertight scroll holder. He had told us that midnight was the right time for tides and the stars would be his guide. I suspect he thought we were an inconvenience and, without a large payment from our new American companion, he might not have piled us on his boat with his already heavy cargo of sisal mats, spices and bananas.

We waded our undignified way to the ancient vessel, keeping haversacks high but allowing sandals, skirts or trousers to become soaked in the warm ocean. We soon sank onto the scratchy sisal mats.

The sailors' work began. The old sail creaked its way up to its full height of forty feet revealing a large hole. A long look at the stars was followed by a good deal of movement of ropes and tying of knots before the sail was adjusted and we were on our way eastwards towards Zanzibar. A platform with a hole in the middle jutting out from the side of the boat behind a high pile of mats was, we were told, for our *abalutions.* Mercifully this was near the back of the boat.

A quiet squeaking confirmed that we were moving and we lay back under the stars munching mini bananas which had cost one Tanzanian shilling for ten. A sudden clattering and splashing turned out to be two dhow-hands using a cooking pot to fill a bucket with which to bail out the unwelcome invasion of puddles under our feet from two sizeable leaks. To stay afloat we would have to take turns throughout the night.

Looking back we could see the palm trees in the moonlight slowly moving away. A stream of moonshine on the water bathed everyone in shimmering silver. Long before we wanted to, we fell asleep amidst the gentle rhythm of movement, creaking and splashing, waking only to do our bailing out duty.

Before dawn we came to a halt as the sails were taken down. The lights of Zanzibar town twinkled five miles away. According to Abdul, if we could trust our Swahili, customs officials would not take too kindly to our creeping into port at dead of dawn.

Fully awake now, we took our grandstand seats to watch the spectacle of the navy blue sky changing to pale blue, then white and finally to a blaze of orange across the water.

The last lap of our journey was through steamers and hundreds of dhows on their way out, perhaps to Dar es Salaam, Mombasa or back to Bagamoyo. Coming into port was sinister. Enormous gun boats and a cargo vessel daubed with oriental script dwarfed our tiny dhow as we slid past.

'Put that camera away,' our American acquaintance

hissed.

After another wait, a motor boat sped out, high foam in its wake. Two uniformed men with fierce expressions leapt on board, frisked the four boys, looked sideways at us girls, thankfully respectfully dressed in long skirts, relieved us of our passports and shot off back to land.

Visions of white slavery weren't alleviated by a piercing whistle wafting across the water and a smaller motor boat chugging out to take us to the shore. The dhow had to find a spot to beach and Abdul couldn't promise to take us back. We hadn't thought that far ahead.

We climbed the steps from the quay to the custom house where we were reunited with our passports and given a pink malaria pill before being ushered straight into two taxis, each held open by a stony-faced police officer.

A short stay in a Zanzibar jail "for our own safety" followed before we were escorted to a designated hotel. Our American "friend" had known about the high-level arms talks between China and Tanzania. Before he disappeared from our hotel that night, he told us he was a CIA agent who had used us as cover. We never saw him again and we never discovered how plane tickets to Nairobi in our names were delivered to our hotel rooms.

A Shift in Time

ALICE AYRES
DAUGHTER OF A BRICKLAYER'S LABOURER
WHO BY INTREPID CONDUCT
SAVED 3 CHILDREN
FROM A BURNING HOUSE
IN UNION STREET BOROUGH
AT THE COST OF HER OWN YOUNG LIFE
APRIL 24 1885

Jane had a set routine for training days at Campbell House. From the turnstiles at Borough Station, turn right by the news-stand and into the Italian cafe. She'd walk past the glass food display and ask for her skinny latte. She never bought her pastry there, not those big overblown things in the display cabinet. With her latte, she'd leave the cafe and cross over the main road. Her first stop was always the newsagent next to Campbell House. She'd smile at the Indian man behind the counter on her right and head left, straight for the rack of croissants and pick up a pecan-lattice pastry with the big silver tweezers. The thought of that fresh, straight-out-of-the-oven smell whenever she stepped inside the shop, made her mouth water. With her Danish in a brown paper bag, she'd pay her 60p and stroll next door through the revolving-doors into the training building. Her fingers would be sticky, her hand already inside the bag, pulling a piece off and putting it in her mouth. Then a sip of latte to wash it down, the two tastes intermingling in her mouth.

Today though, as she came up in the crowded lift at Borough station, she knew she had to hurry. She was not going for training at Campbell House ('Thank God!' she thought). She was going for a routine Occupational Health check, in a building in Union Street, near the corner of Southwark Bridge Road. She'd not be sitting in small groups with people she barely knew, to 'brainstorm' ideas on a piece of flip-chart paper on how to improve the service ('Thank bloody Christ!' she thought again).

That morning, she'd carefully considered what to wear and had put on her good black underwear (she might have to undress for an x-ray – you never knew) and pale, grey, slim-fit slacks, black slip-on mules. Then she'd decided on a long canary-yellow top, and added a thin silver belt. It was a warm summer's day, too hot for a coat. Her blonde hair was pulled back in a black velvet ribbon. She'd wanted to look casual, but fashionable and felt confident she'd succeeded.

In Occupational Health, she would spend half an hour answering questions about her medical history, explain that nasty bout of 'flu from last winter and hopefully that would be it. Afterwards, she was going to meet a former boyfriend for lunch, in the oyster and champagne bar opposite Liverpool Street station, and then return to her office and get on with the backlog of paperwork. She thought about him briefly and sighed. He still wanted to rekindle the dying embers, but she'd moved on. 'No way!' she thought to herself, he was just...well...rather dull. He could buy her a nice lunch and then she'd promise to phone him sometime.

HR would get the Occy Health results, so that her seven days of absence in the last six months would be verified. It was all so ridiculous these days...not as if she was taking months off sick! Anyway, there was just time to get her latte and pecan lattice – about ten minutes to spare! No sense in being early, they'd only keep her sitting in their boring waiting room. She'd already worked out the quickest route to the building, by Googling the post code.

Walking down Marshalsea Road a few minutes later, she sped up as she glanced at her watch and realised she had four minutes to go. She took a swig of her latte and bit into the last chunk of pecan Danish, honey and sugar oozing onto her fingers. A last swallow and there was nothing left in the bag but a pile of flaky crumbs. She sighed, those really were the best pastries anywhere. At the next bin, she dumped the rubbish. Her fingertips were still sticky and she looked around, but no one was close. She licked her fingers and wiped them on a tissue.

At the end of Marshalsea, she turned right into Southwark Bridge Road and walked down towards Union Street. She thought she smelled smoke and lifted her nose to the air and sniffed, just a faint whiff – perhaps there was a bonfire somewhere. Smelt like burning logs. As she reached the corner, she stopped and looked up the road, glancing at the tall buildings on either side counting to herself, 'three, five, seven...must be that one,' she thought and stepped round a bollard towards the curb, waiting to cross.

As she turned, however, her head felt light and she staggered slightly. The air in front of her eyes seemed to shimmer and suddenly the burning smell became overwhelming. She could hear a roar of flames, and blinking, looked over at the building on the other side. She realised she could see flames, licking through the wooden joists of that building.

'What!' She shook her head in total shock. This was not the same street she had looked down a moment ago, surely. Her head turned left, then right, 'What the hell...' She couldn't make any sense of what she was seeing, something was odd about the people around her too, yes, they were all staring at the fire, but look, look at their clothes. The men all had funny black bowler-type hats; the women all had bonnets and long dresses. No-one seemed to be noticing her at all. Even the street was all wrong, it was muddy and rutted, carts pulled by horses were whizzing past her. She jumped back just in time, as the wheel of a fancy carriage just missed her, the nice well-kept wide pavement was gone. She moved back a bit more, letting go a long breath and then looked again at the building that was on fire – it was an old fashioned house, rickety-looking, battered. People were shouting and pointing up to a first floor window – a child, no more than seven, was leaning out, holding onto a toddler and was that another child behind? All were crying for help, but the smoke and flames were billowing up. Who could save them?

She shook her head again, she was either hallucinating or had wandered onto a film set...she couldn't see any cameras though she thought anxiously, scanning the scene. Was that man the director? He seemed to be in charge, pointing and herding the gathering crowd of onlookers. Was anyone going to rescue those kids? The flames looked real enough and so was the smell of burning. The smoke was making her eyes smart.

She looked around again to see if any of these bystanders were going to do something...they were shaking their heads but none was lifting a finger. She wanted to scream at them and then suddenly she saw the young woman, pulling her ginger hair back into a ribbon, tucking her grey dress into her bloomers. She was plump and freckly, big blue eyes, turned-up nose, very Irish looking she thought to herself. The girl was now running forward and into the burning doorway. Jane wanted to scream 'Be careful...' as the girl ran through, but she wouldn't have heard. The girl had a set look on her face, determined. Jane took a step forward slowly, holding her breath. Everyone else seemed to be holding their breath too, waiting. Jane froze for a moment and then heard the crowd gasp, as the girl appeared from the smoky atmosphere, holding one small child under her arm and dragging the other, slightly older, by its hand. The two children stood bedraggled, tear-stained, black streaks on their faces and clothes – the girl thrust them into the arms of a woman standing there.

Now she was turning to go back into the building. Jane shouted to warn her not to go, but her voice came out as a croak. She felt helpless, an observer of the scene, not a participant. A sudden gust of wind sent sparks and smoke flying out from the building into the crowd, who all jumped back, yelling. The woman holding the children was shouting something, her face distraught. Was she the mother?

Again a glimpse of the ginger girl, behind the doorway, this time with another older child! She was shouting something as she propelled the child forward, pushing it towards the now sobbing woman. Just as the child ran out of the doorway, a blackened beam dislodged itself and crashed down in a great shower of sparks and flame. The view was obscured in the pandemonium and smoke, the crowd groaned. Jane stood on tiptoes, straining to see. Oh, she hoped the ginger girl got out. Did she? She found her cheeks were wet, but all she could see was the crowd backing away as the conflagration in front of them took further hold.

The girl's absence had stunned the now subdued crowd. The mother, if that's who she was, clutched the three children clinging to her long skirts. All appeared to be wailing, their faces contorted, staring towards the burning building. The mother's hand was outstretched – were there more children inside? Or had the ginger girl been a relative?

The man she had thought was the movie director, she now realised, was wearing some kind of dark uniform and carried a helmet. He was holding the woman's arm, pulling her and the children away from the scene. The woman looked dazed as she turned away, her head drooped and her arms fell hopelessly, encircling the children.

Jane felt giddy again as the sadness of the scene overwhelmed her. She shook her head trying to clear it, searched her pocket for a tissue to wipe her watering eyes. She felt a steadying hand on her arm and looked up. A woman was smiling at her. 'Are you alright?' she said. The woman was dressed in a dark business suit, short skirt, green-glazed beads around her neck, pointed shoes. Jane stared at her, as if she was an apparition. Looking over the woman's shoulder, she saw tall buildings, a wide street and a black London cab dropping off a fare. She pulled the tissue out of her pocket and dabbed at her eyes.

'Yes, yes, thank you...I'm fine', she said. 'No, really, I must have got something in my eye'.

The woman half-smiled uncertainly.

'Are you sure?'

'Yes, yes! I'm sure,' she said, arranging her face into a smile. She just wanted the woman to go away and leave her to think.

'Thank you!' she said firmly.

The woman shrugged and walked on and Jane looked carefully at the street. She steadied herself, putting her hand on a lamp post. She squeezed her eyes shut, then opened them again. No! The scene was still the same. She sniffed the air – surely she could still smell a faint whiff of burning wood? It must be her imagination. The whole thing was her imagination. Or was it a hallucination? There must be a reasonable explanation? She'd better not mention it to anyone, they'd think she'd flipped. Imagine what the doc in Occupational Health would say? She shuddered at the thought. She glanced at her watch and was shocked to discover it said ten o'clock. That meant...no time had passed since the whole thing happened. She frowned, feeling confused. She was on time for her appointment. It felt like hours had passed. She sighed, then straightened and put her shoulders back, crossing the road.

Number seven was a tall black-glazed building and as she pushed open the big glass door and stepped towards the semi-circular reception desk, her heart skipped a beat. The receptionist, a plump red-head, with her hair pulled back and freckles on her turned-up nose, smiled.

Expedients

'It's just...so much...'
　'I get that.'
　'I didn't understand why she kept it to herself for so many years.'
　　'Your mother was protecting you.'
　　'I can't believe you agreed to it.'
　　'Mind if I touch you?'
　'It was selfish – both of you.'
　'She said you have my jaw and mouth. I see...she's right.'
　'Did you ever think what would've been the best for me?'
　'One could only accept.'
　'I was shocked to find she was my birth mother.'
　'You grazed yourself on the knee the last time we were here in the park.'
　'Didn't she have any qualms about leaving you behind?'
　'"It's time to face the music," she said. She was right.'
　'I used to wonder who my father was.'
　'She had her duties. I had mine, too.'
　'To think of her coming home with an "orphan"... who was actually her own child.'
　'It was complicated...'
　'She was using you.'
　'I had the means and I loved both of you very much. It was best to let you go.'
　'It was hard for me.'
　'You're still angry with us.'
　'I need to know more.'
　'I – we, managed to arrange your adoption in due course. We wouldn't have done had it not been obvious because of your marble skin and blue Nile eyes. What would've your people thought of...'
　'I wasn't worth the embarrassment, was I?'
　'We didn't want you to be judged by anyone.'
　'You had no idea.'
　'I'm sure she didn't let you down.'
　'Did she write after we settled down in Jakarta?'
　'She didn't.'

'You didn't...mind?'

'It was extremely hard for me. Wondering what became of you and not watching you grow up.'

'For years I wished I wasn't different from others – my dark-skinned friends...'

'Naturally, darling. But I never forgot you.'

'I would've liked you to find me.'

'At times, things are best remaining as they are.'

'When I read her letter, after...the accident...'

'It must've been awful.'

'Devastating. The fact that she insisted on being called 'tante;' I can't imagine doing that to my own child. Four years have gone and the pain is still raw...'

'I'm so pleased she contacted me – six months before her death. As if she realised she hadn't had much time.'

'I wondered why she'd stayed single.'

'She was very beautiful. Smart and sharp, too. By the way, I've brought all the documents – you can have them.

'Perhaps only *Eyang Kakung,* er, Grandpa, knew that something was untoward.'

'She told me a lot about him; he seemed to be a very wise man, wasn't he?'

'Quite. He might've realised that there were far too many similarities between his daughter and her "adopted" child.'

'About your *status*... if you wish to change it, you can.'

'You said yourself it's better to leave things as they are.'

'The end of the sixties wasn't suitable for single mothers. You would've been taken into care had we not been married.'

'I'm aware of them because she mentioned it in the letter. I thought it was only Indonesians who are concerned about "papers".'

'We did what we could to keep the two of you together.'

'Thirty-five years...'

They talk for a little more outside a cafe at Hyde Park. Then they become silent; she looks away with blurry eyes, watching her husband chasing their toddler by the lake. She sighs as she conjures up in her mind similar memories; waving goodbye to a tall man in a suit whose gaze followed her as she was walking away with her mother. Having whimpered a little because of the throbbing pain in her grazed knee, she was too little to understand that she would not see him again for a very long time.

The man takes a large brown folder from his satchel – the yellowing papers on his daughter's history. Later she will read how an English man and a poor Indonesian PhD student married in secret three months before the baby was born. When she finished her thesis four years afterwards, she brought the child back to her native country and closed the London chapter of her life.

'I'm glad we've met at last,' he remarks. She reaches for his hand and squeezes it; the way she remembers his squeezing hers moments before they parted years ago.

The Dream Car

The woman stood rigid. Her senses were stripped bare, peeled back by the skinning amber strobes and the sing-song sirens of the vans. She felt no pain. Only when a young policeman came with comfort did her legs betray her. She fell down heavily. But before they could hold her, pick her up from the tarmac, grief strode in to seize the limp doll and shake and shake until the last salt pearls of its joy were dusted out.

They unfolded a sheet, thin and silver, to keep her warm. It was then that the girl came up to stand at her side. Pale and shivering in a white night-gown, she was wrapped in her own blanket of grey, coarse wool. Tears streamed from her pale green eyes, tears which the woman could not cry, as together they watched the little car burn.

Once before they had stood like this, on a night like this, when smoke and flames were all around. There had been high planes in a searchlight sky and a slow, low thudding of faraway guns. Then the girl had stood white, pure white against a dark window, waiting for a climbing fireman to take her into his arms. He had taken her, taken her down, onto his steep ladder's rungs where his groping hand had reached into the white linen of her innocence to purge all trust. Then she had stood alone; alone and sobbing beside the soaring ladders of her guilt, until a woman stepped out from the weeping girl, to smother the child in the thick blanket of her shame. When the mother came they had both run back to the trembling breast where they were safe again, yet nothing was said.

Time passed and there was a new home and a general store with a ringing till which fed them all. And the grown woman took on the shop when the mother died and she hid the girl in the cans and brown boxes on the vinegared shelves. One day something stirred, deep, deep down and the woman turned to stare at the wall. So she had picked out the time and found the stranger, she gave him drinks and all that he wanted. She had turned appalled from his beery breath, from his fumbling grasp to endure at last the fierce thrust of his thighs. But she smiled. And she took the seed and she kept it safe. And the seed grew and the woman grew and the neighbours' curtains stirred as she walked by with her belly bulging, yet nothing was said.

A child burst out and cried in the light. The girl and the woman saw their daughter and they laughed and they wept. The young child grew and happiness grew in the corner-shopped corner of their little world. Joy flowed and every day the sun came in with open door smiles. And there were sand pies and dancing on wide sea shores. The woman stared at the blazing car and saw again a stilted pier set stark on the sand against a bright red sky. And the girl sobbed on her lonely hard shoulder.

Then there were badges and blazers. A bright young scholar stood up to stand out at school and university. The woman was proud. She bought a car, and learned to drive, to ferry them up to the far off town. The car was theirs and they all stretched back, dreaming and glad as it plied between cloister and home.

The little car purred as it sped on back to the smoke grey town. When it suddenly stopped, the woman got out to run to the kerb-side phone to ask for help. She had turned to see the juggernaut, to see it sweep down with its Jericho horns and pulsing lights. It had rammed the car, brushed it along like a match and the cab reared up to smash hard down, hungry for blood and the first born flesh.

Firemen came with acetylene blades to lance away the folded roof but their daughter was dead. Gently they took her out. They all drew back as the flames crept down from the smouldering cab and they shielded their faces as the red nest grew.

Wrapped in her cloak, the mute woman stared. A fireman came up with an axe in his belt. He knelt at her side. He laid his white heavy gloves down on the ground and unscrewed the top of a silver flask. But the woman shrank back.

'Take it! Take it!' screamed the girl. 'I want to go!'

So she took the cup with the strong sweet tea and drank deep until his steady-now, easy-now hands drew it back. As the steam cleared she saw the girl go skipping along the concrete lane and climb into the car to lie in its flames.

Katie Alford

Katie is a computer graduate who currently works and resides in London. She excels at starting novels but is not so good at finishing them, with her works in progress now into double figures. In addition to writing she is also a digital artist, specialising in 3D environment modelling. The current genres she has written works in include fantasy, sci-fi, steampunk, dark fantasy, folklore and detective. She has won a number of short story competitions. She is very excited to be working with publisher, Kristell Ink, on her novel *Atlantis and the Game of Time*.
Twitter: @Katie_alford1

June Armstrong-Wright

June came to fiction writing via many years of working in radio for Radio Television Hong Kong, Public Broadcasting Service in America and the BBC in London. Her career also encompasses acting, directing and writing for the theatre in these three parts of the world. She wrote and directed a play on the life and times of Henrietta Barnett and is currently working on 'A Peek over the Privets', a light-hearted entertainment for gardeners.

Lindsay Bamfield

Lindsay is a co-founder of Greenacre Writers. She has completed her first novel, and is working on her second. She has written several short stories and flash-fiction pieces, some of which have won prizes. She has had work published in *Mslexia, Writing Magazine, Words With Jam* and in anthologies including *Voices from the Web* and *The Best of Café Lit 2012*. She has also contributed non-fiction articles to the e-zine: In The Powderroom. Lindsay fits her writing around her career as a specialist speech and language therapist.
Blog: www.lindsaybamfield.blogspot.co.uk
Twitter: @LindsayBamfield

Veronica Bright

Veronica has been a storyteller for as long as she can remember, a skill which came in handy when she worked as a primary school teacher with delightful, bouncy and

exhausting 4 and 5 year olds. The children inspired her to write short plays now published by Kevin Mayhew as *Frogs in Assembly* and *Robots in Assembly*. Since retiring she has won a string of prizes for her short stories. She is currently seeking representation for her novel for 8-12 year olds, and is working on her first novel for adults. She says she learns something every time she writes a new story. Veronica writes a monthly series of tips for new writers on her website.
Website: www.veronicabright.co.uk
Twitter: @BrightVeronica

Andrew Byrne

Andrew is the author of *Some Place South of Perfect*, a tale of interweaving lives set in contemporary London. Having moved to London from Ireland in the mid-80s, he worked in the City for over 20 years. He writes a blog, *Word Watching*, in which the OED is a place populated by living words. Andrew lives with his wife in Muswell Hill, North London, where he is a member of the WEA Writing for Pleasure group.
Blog: www.wordwatching1.blogspot.co.uk
Twitter: @andybyrne363

Rosie Canning

Rosie lives in London. As co-founder of Greenacre Writers she runs 'Start That Novel' workshops and writers' retreats. Her short stories have been short-listed and published, the most recent being a 100 word flash-fiction 'Uncoupled' on the Café Lit website. She has written a non-fiction book *Occupied and Opened - the story of Friern Barnet Library* and contributed a chapter to *Steering the Mothership: The Complexities of Mothering* by Lisa Cherry, Spring Publishing (2014). She is currently having great fun re-inventing her life in *Hiraeth*, an autobiographical novel about a 16-year-old care leaver who is addicted to fiction.
Blog: www.rosemarycanning.blogspot.co.uk
Twitter: @Rosie_Canning

Ruth Cohen

Ruth says she wrote bad poetry in her twenties but returned to writing prose after she retired. She has written short stories and flash-fiction, and has been published in previous anthologies. Her working background was in careers counselling, and after reading English at UCL she joined the ILEA, subsequently heading up services in the University of the Arts and City University. She is currently attempting her first novel which she dreams one day of finishing. She lives in Finchley with her supportive partner Rob.

Bettina von Cossel

Bettina writes novels and short stories, mainly in German. Since finding a dead body under her hotel window as a teenager, and a bloody knife in the upholstery of a chair she is hooked on crime writing. So far, five of her crime novels have been published in Germany, and well over a hundred short stories. Bettina lives in London, together with her husband, four children and a dog.

Cecilia Crowson

Cecilia started writing for her own enjoyment, joining her local Grace Dieu Writers Circle when she retired nearly two years ago. Apart from having one story short-listed, and one commended, this story is her first success, but then she has entered only a handful of competitions so far. She is intermittently working on a series of short stories connected by a common family relationship.

Linda Louisa Dell

Linda has published articles, short stories and over ten books including three non-fiction self-help books: *Can't Sleep, Won't Sleep; Dreamtime* and *Aphrodite's Secrets* and three novels: *African Nights; Yes, and Pigs Might Fly,* (runner-up in the Wishing Shelf best fiction awards in 2012); and the latest: *Earthscape: a Long Way from Home.*
Website: www.lindalouisadell.com

Jo Derrick

Jo has numerous short stories and articles published in a wide range of publications, including *Mslexia, Writers' Forum, Woman's Weekly Fiction Special, Take A Break's Fiction Feast, Upstart!, Peninsular, Buzzwords, The Whittaker Prize Anthology.* She has recently published an e-book of her prize-winning short stories, *Twisted Sheets* which is available via

Amazon on Kindle. Jo is the former editor/publisher of *The Yellow Room Magazine*, a print journal for women writers, which recently folded, and former publisher of *QWF Magazine*. She has written a psychological crime novel and is now working on a historical novel.
Twitter: @yellowjo

Eliza Jane Goés

Eliza Jane retired from teaching in 2006 and now has time to scribble even more than before. Her background as a teacher in Africa, and in multicultural Hendon School encouraged her to write about positive and enriching cross cultural encounters. Her trilogy of novels *Fusion, The Cosmopolites* and *The Not Quite English Teacher* are fictionalised memoirs on the theme of migration leading to cultural integration and a global view of the world. Her manuscript *Cyber Spooks*, for 9-12 year olds, with illustrations by Gina Rahman, is almost ready to submit for publication. She is appreciative of support from Greenacre Writers.
Blog: www.elizajanegoesahead.com
Twitter: @Elizajanego

Shirley Golden

Much of Shirley's work lurks in the recesses of her laptop where it awaits further coffee-fuelled sessions of juggling words. Some of her short fiction pieces have found homes in the pages of magazines and anthologies or in various corners of the internet; a few have won prizes. She can often be found on Twitter when she should be writing.
Website: www.shirleygolden.net
Twitter: @shirl1001

Anna Meryt

Anna had her first poem – about the Vietnam War – published in her convent school magazine. Anna, a performance poet, is a member of Highgate Poets, in North London. Many of her poems are published in poetry magazines and anthologies, including *The West In Her Eye, Her Mind's Eye,* and Highgate Poets' 2013 anthology. In 2011 she won first prize in the Lupus International poetry competition for her poem *Bulawayo* – her birth place. Her first poetry pamphlet,

Heartbroke, was published last year and *Dolly Mix*, her second collection, was published recently. Anna has also completed her first book – a memoir set in South Africa in the 1970s, *A Hippopotamus at The Table*.
Blog: www.amerytpoetryetc.blogspot.co.uk
Twitter: @ameryt

Mumpuni Murniati

Murni grew up in Java, Indonesia. She was short-listed in *Litro's* Dutch Short Story Competition in 2012. She likes landscape photography, makes delicious spring rolls and Singapore Laksa and can swim four-hundred metres in less than ten minutes. She is married and has three young children.

David Nixon

David has lived in London for forty years. He is an architect; as well as winning awards for buildings in glass and steel, his practice has worked in green oak, notably at Shakespeare's Globe. He also farms in North Staffordshire where his close affinity with the land inspires much of his short fiction and poetry. He is a founder member of the Bloomsbury writing group Liber8 and is currently working on his first novel.

Sal Page

Sal has a Creative Writing MA from Lancaster University. She won the Calderdale Short Story Prize in 2011 and has numerous stories published both online and in print publications including *Jawbreakers, Greenacre Writers Anthology Volume 1, Stories for Homes* and *The Pygmy Giant.* She's been placed in several competitions and short-listed in many more. She is currently writing her second novel, *Curls*, while looking for an agent for her first novel *Queen of the World.*
Blog: www.sal-cobbledtogether.blogspot.co.uk
Twitter: @SalnPage

The Greenacre Project

The Greenacre Project is a North London non-profit community group that was set up in 2007. We promote community values, sustainable living including sustainable transport with an emphasis on cycling. We value local green spaces and work to raise awareness about nature, trees and wildlife. We also promote health and wellbeing through creativity.

The Greenacre Project published a local community magazine *The Greenacre Times,* with a variety of articles on the issues we support as well as humanitarian concerns worldwide, environmental matters, health and wellbeing and local history.

Members of The Greenacre Project have been involved in a number of local nature preservation days in our wonderful green spaces. We organized five successful Bicycle Rallies in the Borough of Barnet and now organize guided walks charting the miles of footpaths and interesting green spaces and water features. We also hold the Greenacre Film Club showing slideshows and films about community and environmental ventures, and host talks from a variety of speakers on the topics we are promoting.

Greenacre Writers hold three thriving writing groups and various creative writing workshops, open to all. We have held three international short story competitions and the first two Greenacre Writers Literary Festivals have expanded to the larger more inclusive Finchley Literary Festival.

The Greenacre Project

www.greenacreproject.blogspot.com

e-mail: greenacreproject@gmail.com

Greenacre Writers

www.greenacrewriters.blogspot.com

e-mail: greenacrewriters@gmail.com

Twitter @GreenacreWriter

Finchley Literary Festival

e-mail: finchleyliteraryfestival@gmail.com

Twitter @FinchleyLitFest